THE BUSHIDO CHRONICLES

BOOK ONE
COMING HOME

BY
JASON BRICK

Cover design:
Interior design: Anita Jones, Another Jones Graphics

ISBN: 978-1-938445-12-5

CHAPTER ONE

Coach Russel used the F-word. Twice.

He sat two chairs down from me, his face as red as … well, nothing's as red as Coach's face when he's really swole up. Apples aren't that red. He cussed in that loud stage whisper coaches use so only their athletes can hear what they're saying. On the mat, Jordan Walker kicked his legs and struggled, flat on his back with a kid from Washington High on top of him.

Jordan rolled out quickly, but being on your back costs points. A minute later, it turned out to be enough points to cost him the match. Coach swore again. The scoreboard switched to Ponderosa 38, Washington 40. They'd gained the lead for the first time all night.

Here's how it is in wrestling. You use moves to score points against the other guy while the other guy uses different moves to score points against you. The one with the most points at the end of three rounds wins. Sometimes you hold him on his back long enough to get a "pin." For tournament matches, that's mostly all that matters. In a dual meet — one school against the other — how your match turns out scores points for the team. If you win, that's three points for your side. Get pinned, and that's six for theirs.

I scanned the bleachers for about the hundredth time. I knew Mom was working her shift at the ER tonight. There were so few nurses compared to the need that she always had to work extra shifts, but sometimes she found a way to be there.

She also had to work a lot because of my dad. Some people say we Maori have a genetic tendency for trouble with alcohol and drugs. I don't know about Maori in general, but my dad sure has a problem. We owed a lot of people a lot of money when Mom moved us away from him, and we still owed most of it. I knew I was important to her, but so was eating. And sleeping indoors. She wouldn't be in the bleachers tonight.

But that didn't mean I wouldn't look for her.

Jordan trudged past me, his headgear hanging loose in one hand. I slugged him in the shoulder. "Good effort, Walker."

From the bench behind me, where the second-string team sat, Mario DuPree sneered. "Yeah, Jordan. Way to win it for the other guys."

"How many points did you score tonight, DuPree?" my mouth said before my brain could stop it. I didn't want trouble with him or anybody else, just wanted to wrestle and mind my own business. I'd only been at Ponderosa High for three weeks, and history said I'd move again before spring break. Still, I hate to see anybody kicked when they're down. I had to say something.

DuPree stood up, hard and fast. He was a senior, and the heavyweight varsity spot had been his for the past two years. Then I came along a month into the season and beat him in a qualifying match. That made me the varsity guy, and stuck him riding a bench.

Coach's arm snaked between us, "DuPree! Morgan! Belay that. Both of you. Right now."

We sat down. There was none of that mad-dog staring or facing off you get sometimes, not with Coach right there. DuPree did kick the back of my chair as soon as Coach looked away, but that sort of thing doesn't matter. You get used to it.

Bam! Out on the mat, Sage Kaiser pinned her opponent in less time than it took for DuPree to put his foot down. Sage was the only girl on our varsity lineup. She stood six-foot-two in her socks and wrestled in the 220-pound division. Sage jogged off the mat and high-fived Coach. The score moved to 44–40. We were back in the lead.

I strapped on my headgear and jogged to the center of the mat. A short brick of a kid with muscles like something out of a comic book jogged out to meet me. Part of me felt nervous, but my breath came slow and easy. I knew how to push that part away, focus on the job in front of me.

We shook hands. The ref put the whistle to his lips. Time slowed into a perfect moment, stretching on a tightrope of tension, apprehension and potential. The whistle blew.

Round one rolled by in a slow dance of attempted tackles and throws, most unsuccessful. In the last seconds, I managed a hip toss for a weak takedown. The kid from Washington escaped almost instantly. The buzzer sounded, and we broke with me leading 2--1.

He won the coin toss and deferred choice of position to me. That forced me to pick now so he could choose at the beginning of the final round. It would give him a strategic advantage. I chose down position, where he had a better chance of pinning me but I had more opportunities to score points.

I shot forward and stood up the instant the whistle blew, popping out of my opponent's grip and scoring an escape. Three to one, me leading. I shot in low while he was still off balance, swept his legs up and out from under him, landed on top and kept him down. He tried to flip me off his back while I searched for a chance to get the pin. For 90 seconds, neither of us got what we wanted. The round ended with me leading, 5–1.

He took down position for the third round, hoping to score with an escape or reversal. I hit him hard when the whistle blew, reaching deep across his stomach to trap his wrist. He pinned my arm with his other hand and rolled, taking me up and over his shoulder. I landed hard on my back with him on top of me. By the time I caught my breath, he was lying across my chest with one arm wrapped tightly around my neck and arm.

All of his weight ground into my chest while his biceps and forearm squeezed both sides of my neck. It hurt, and breathing hurt even more. I tried to bridge up, but that just pushed my throat into the muscles of his chest. I choked and fell back. Lying back and letting the pin happen would be so easy. All the pain would go away.

"Short time!" I heard a voice shout from our side of the mat. I couldn't tell whose.

A pin would score six points for Washington and we would lose. If I suffered for just a few more seconds, they'd get only the three for beating me. We'd win.

"Short time, Morgan! Short time!" More voices, from seemingly far away. It sounded like the whole team, maybe even DuPree. I bit my teeth together and rolled up onto my head into a high hard bridge. My back arched up off the mat, but the move cut off my windpipe so I couldn't breathe. Little stars danced across my vision, between me and the gym ceiling. My chest hurt. My neck hurt. My back started to shudder from the effort of keeping the arch high off the mat.

"Short time!" voices came from the stands now, too, everyone telling me the match was almost over, that I only had to hold on for a few more seconds. This is why I joined the team even when I knew I'd probably leave before end of season. When you move all the time, you don't make real friends. At that moment, though, everybody had my back. They all cared what I did and what happened to me. It was a real connection, a place for me to belong, even if it would be over as soon as the buzzer rang.

Even my eyes hurt as the blood throbbed in my face. Washington tried to kick my legs out from under me, and that hurt my shins and calves. I bit down harder and focused everything I had on keeping daylight between my back and the ground. Well, on that and not screaming or passing out from the pain.

The buzzer sounded. The ref separated us. With the five points from his reversal and near fall, Washington won the match. The team score finished at Ponderosa 44, Washington 43. We shook hands and the ref raised the Washington kid's arm above our heads. He'd won our battle, but I'd done my part to win the war.

I jogged back to my seat, my lungs still burning from the ordeal. I always jog, no matter what happened in the match, no matter how tired or hurt or discouraged I am. It's a matter of principle.

Coach Russel gripped my hand and looked me in the eyes. "You were better than him, Morgan."

"I know, Coach." It was all I could say. He was right, and we both knew it.

"You got careless. You let him sucker you."

"I'm sorry, Coach. It won't happen again."

"I know. Way to tough it out."

"Thanks."

"Seriously, that's one armpit I wouldn't spend time in for love or money." I laughed. Coach smiled. We both joined the lineup to shake hands with the other team.

We walked out of the gym in a straight line, disciplined but relaxed. From the back bench, DuPree gave me a hard look, staring at me like, well, like I'd just stolen his spot on the varsity team. I got the message that he'd want to talk with me at length about that, and probably sometime soon.

As usual, the hall between the gym and the locker room was fully crazy. It was like that at every school I'd ever been to. Wrestling isn't as popular as football or basketball, but our team was doing well this year. Students and parents crowded around, high-fiving the night's champions and wishing buddies well. Girlfriends, dads and moms waited to congratulate or console. Friends ran around contributing to the general chaos.

Unlike usual, Susan Parker was leaning against the wall between a drinking fountain and a staff office door. She wore a yellow "Ponderosa" T-shirt, and her brown ponytail stuck out through the gap in her ball cap.

Susan.

Freaking.

Parker.

Susan Freaking Parker from my second-period English class. Susan F. Parker with the long brown hair and grey eyes like something out of a song. Susan Parker with those freckles, and that laugh, and legs like you only ever see on champion track runners. Which she was.

Susan Freaking Parker looked right at me. I tried not to choke. She pushed herself off the wall and started walking beside me. Right. Next. To. Me.

And I'd thought my heart was pounding out on the mat.

"I saw your match tonight," she said.

"Saw me get my rear end kicked," I said.

"But didn't you win the match for our team? I saw how hard you fought to not get pinned. If you hadn't stuck it out, we'd have lost."

Butterflies fought with light sabers in my stomach. Unless I'd heard wrong, that sounded like a compliment from Susan Parker. I must have heard wrong. My palms started to sweat. I wanted to say something clever, but my brain wasn't working. It was too busy shouting at me about how Susan Freaking Parker was walking right next to me, apparently on purpose.

"Wow," I managed. "You know a lot about wrestling for a girl."

She punched me in the arm. Hard. "That's a very sexist thing to say."

I liked her even more for saying that and for the punch, if such a thing were possible. "Uh, I'm sorry. I meant. Um ..."

But Susan smiled. It was the brightest thing I'd seen maybe ever. "Do you have any particular place to be later tonight?"

"Not until midnight," I said. "My mom comes home from work then, and I like to be home to check in on her."

"You check in on your mom?"

"Um, yes?" Mom was the only family I had, and we each did our part to keep the other safe.

"She doesn't check in on you? You really are the epic Neanderthal, aren't you?"

I blushed all over my face and arms. One nice thing about having dark skin is you can blush and white people don't usually notice. On the other hand, my mouth wasn't working at all. We were just a few steps from the locker room door, and I couldn't think of a way to rescue the situation.

Susan rescued it for me. "We can go to Shari's if you want. I'll wait out here."

Shari's is a 24-hour restaurant with lots of locations in Oregon, like a local chain version of Denny's. It's open all night, and it isn't a bar, so it's the go-to late-night food choice for most Ponderosa students.

"Um, okay," I said. *Idiot,* I thought. *You faced off against a 260-pound monster who almost took your head home in his gym bag, and you can't even talk to this girl?*

The locker room doors swung shut behind me. I took my first real breath since seeing Susan in the hallway and wondered if I could ever make myself go back out there.

CHAPTER TWO

Jordan Walker was on the other side of the door, already dressed in his street clothes and ready to go. "Hey, Morgan," he said with a goofy grin. He bobbed his eyebrows like that guy with the mustache from all those old movies. "Was that Susan Parker with you in the hall?"

My stomach butterflies resurged. Susan Freaking Parker. "Um, yeah. I guess."

"Way to go, man. Seriously."

"Um, thanks." I couldn't even say something clever to Jordan. How could I hope to impress Susan? I was doomed.

"Dude, party at my house. My parents are home, so no beer or hooking up. But some movies. Snacks. Acting stupid 'cause we won. Like that."

"Sounds good," I said.

"Hey, I understand if you have better things to do." He made a rude gesture with his hips when he said "better things."

"It's not like that, Jordan."

"Not like that *yet*, you mean."

"Come on, man. It's really not like that."

"Whatever you say, Connor. But I'm pretty sure she'll decide what it's like. Anyway, show up if she stiffs you."

"Thanks. I will." I said it because I wanted out of the conversation, not because I wanted to go. Jordan's not bad, but if I ended up alone tonight I didn't think I'd be in the mood for company. Besides, it was best not to get too close. Moving hurts less when you keep things at a distance.

The shower felt good — hot water on muscles already aching from my match. I soaped up and rinsed off, smelled my pits and soaped up again. I hadn't thought to bring any deodorant, and I had a first date as soon as I got dressed. No toothbrush, either, and my mouth had been in that guy's armpit for at least a minute. Maybe if I just stayed in the shower until Susan got bored and went home. That would probably be best for everybody.

I forced myself out by turning the water all the way to cold, which made my bod leap away whether or not my brain wanted to move. I shivered and shook as I toweled off, a little from the cold but mostly because I was one step closer to embarrassing myself with Susan Parker.

Susan Freaking Parker. Why couldn't it have been some other girl at the school? Somebody I wouldn't care so much about looking like an idiot in front of. It would be like a practice session before a match.

I was toweling off my hair when Mr. Keranovak, the school's head janitor, wheeled his mop bucket past my row of lockers. He did a double-take when he saw me.

"Are you all right? Just about everybody else is gone."

"Yes sir, I'm fine. I've just got no place to go. I'm not in any hurry." Maybe Susan had gone home already, so I wouldn't be telling a lie.

"Fair enough," he said. Mr. Keranovak's accent wasn't thick, but you could hear it in his vowels. He stretched them out of shape with every syllable. "You did good tonight. The way that kid was squeezing your neck like wringing a towel. It was hard to watch."

"Thanks," I said.

"Really. You're a tough kid."

That helped my nerves a little. Rumor was, Mr. Keranovak grew up in a war zone and got his U.S. citizenship by serving in the Marine Corps. He was some kind of hero. I'd never thought of myself as tough, but Mr. Keranovak would know it when he saw it.

The janitor poked his mop handle in my direction. He said "Nice ink."

"Huh?"

"On your shoulder, kid. What is that, kanji? Like from Japan? I was stationed at Sasebo for a while, and it looks like that."

I thought about the collection of red, raised lines on my right shoulder blade. They formed the shape of a box above a row of smaller marks, visible to me only if I stood facing a mirror just the right way. I'd never thought of it before, but I could see what Mr. Keranovak meant. It did kind of look like the tattoos you saw college girls get on their backs and ankles.

"No," I said. "It's a birthmark."

His head did a funny jerk and his eyebrows popped wider with surprise. Surprise and something else, something darker. Maybe he thought I was lying.

"Really?" he said.

"Really."

"Fair enough. Anyway, you showed real grit tonight. You're more dangerous than people give you credit for."

"Thanks, Mr. Keranovak."

"You earned it." One of the little plastic wheels squeaked as he wheeled his mop bucket out of sight.

I scrubbed myself dry. If everybody was already gone, Susan had probably given up. My rolling stomach hoped so, but at the same time the rest of me hoped not. Against all odds, she seemed interested in talking with me. I tried to hurry into my clothes. It was a nervous hurry, the worst kind. My big toe caught in the waistband of my underwear and I barely saved myself from falling on my face.

When I steadied myself, DuPree was standing at the end of the row of lockers. Arturo Mendez and Ivan Cummings stood behind and to either side of him. DuPree's two friends were both kind of short and kind of fat, but they were that kind of fat where you know there's plenty of muscle underneath. The nerves came back to my stomach, harder and sharper than when I thought of Susan. I dropped my jeans and backed down the aisle, still in just my tighty whities.

The three walked toward me. None of them said anything.

"What's up, guys?" The words came out in a high squeak as my throat shut tight with fear. I darted looks to my left and right looking for Mr. Keranovak, but he was gone. I was on my own.

DuPree, Arturo and Ivan stalked toward me. They still hadn't said a word or looked anywhere but directly at me. The room darkened as they came near. Their shadows seemed to writhe on the floor and benches.

I felt the electric zing of real fear. After years of moving into new schools, I know bullies. You'd think being as big as I am would be some protection, but you'd think wrong. A new big guy is either a threat or a trophy. Either way, the local wildlife has to sniff around for a while when you show up. Bullies are loud. They want to make fun, to show off. They want everybody to see what they do to you. Walking up all quiet like this wasn't how bullies acted.

It was how killers acted.

I backed up further until my rear hit the wall at the end of the aisle. My hands started to shake. My mind got fuzzy, filling with a cloud of panic, making me see things that couldn't really be happening.

Behind DuPree, the shadows seemed to stretch and morph into impossible shapes. DuPree's looked like some kind of bird, all long and spindly with a wickedly sharp beak. Arturo's shadow grew fatter and fatter until it blotted out the floor all around him. Ivan's looked like a badger, or an angry dog, bristling and quivering with terrible energy.

DuPree raised up his hands. Not like a boxer would, but with his fingers apart and toward me like claws. Or talons.

I screamed. It wasn't a mighty battle cry, much as I'd like to say it was. More like a frightened teenager about to run for his life. Which is what I did, breaking left and shoulder-checking Ivan with a wrenching crunch. He grunted, stumbled into DuPree's path and the two of them fell into a tangled heap. I hopped up onto a bench and skipped past the knot of thugs before they could react. They were big like me, but I was faster. I slammed into the locker room door and out into the hall.

Susan was leaning against the opposite wall, sipping Coke out of a plastic bottle. It fell from her hand when she saw me. In my underwear. Running away.

CHAPTER THREE

"Hi, Susan," I squeaked.

"What the weird?" she squeaked back.

The locker room doors flew open behind me and I ran for the exit. If I could outpace DuPree and his gang, maybe I could double back. I could put on some clothes and find help. There had to be some kind of adult around, even at night. Mr. Keranovak, maybe. This didn't feel right, the way those guys were acting, not like it would if DuPree was just taking a shot at me for what happened with his varsity slot. This was something else. Something worse.

On the bright side, getting killed by three teenage sociopaths would mean I didn't have to look Susan in the eye after what just happened.

I hit the exit doors with all three of them hot on my tail. Susan screamed, but I was already through and out into the wet January night. Just kept running while the girl stood there in harm's way. My pursuers didn't seem interested in her, though, so the farther away I got the safer she would be. They ran after me, faster now than they'd been in the locker room.

The pavement scraped my bare feet as I ran in the winter dark, then came cool, wet grass. I sprinted across the soccer fields, gaining a little distance. Their footfalls squished behind me fading a little with every step. If I could keep going, I might outgas the two shorter ones. Maybe I could handle DuPree alone in a fair fight. I'd handled him on the mat. But I didn't want to fight. This whole thing was too scary, too weird.

I ran harder across the grass, shooting beneath the tall floodlights installed to prevent crime. Crime like assault and murder, I hoped. The fence at the edge of the grounds loomed up in the dark, right in front of me. DuPree was too close behind for me to climb over. He'd catch me before I could get out of reach. I cut left, running along the line of the fence.

It curved at an angle, forming a dead end like three sides of a stop sign. The baseball diamond. I would have seen it in time during daylight, but I didn't know the new school well enough to navigate my just the floodlights. There would be gaps for the dugouts I could squirm through, but I couldn't spot them in the darkness. If I guessed wrong, DuPree and his gang would be on top of me before I could recover.

Behind me DuPree, Arturo and Ivan had slowed to a walk and spread out wide enough to catch me if I tried to run past them. No escape that direction. In front of me, the fences were too high, the school too far away. I was trapped.

I faced them and backed into the batting area until my rear hit the chain of the backstop. My hands gripped the links as my body pressed against it, squeezing the cold metal tight. I knew they'd start shaking if I let go. DuPree walked straight at me. The others closed in from either side. None of them said a word.

"Okay, guys," my voice shook so much I could see little waves in the vapor coming out of my mouth. "Joke's over. You really got me."

Nothing from any of them. Not a word. Not a smirk. Not even a satisfied grunt for catching me after all the trouble. Their shadows writhed and danced on the ground, darker than should have been possible under the distant floodlights, still in the weird animal shapes I'd seen in the locker room.

"Mario, man," I screamed, "Enough's enough. You got me."

They stepped closer, their crazy shadows seeming to suck the light out of the air around us. DuPree's birdlike shade spread its wings so it covered most of the infield. It eclipsed the other shadows, covering the field in darkness.

"Coach will be really ticked off if you do what I think you're thinking of. Seriously, man."

In one more step, DuPree would be close enough to reach out and touch me. My gut clenched in knots. I could feel the sand beneath my feet, each individual grain. The shadows grew thicker still.

"What are you going to do?" I shouted. I took a wrestling stance. It's not the best stance for a real fight, but it's the one I knew. With three against one, I probably didn't have much chance anyway.

No movie of my life ran in front of my eyes. Instead, I thought about my mom, and Susan Parker, and winning a state championship. It was more like the life I wouldn't get to live flashed through my head.

With the three huge enemies in front of me, I wished for the power of Maui, a hero from Maori legend. The stories say he beat the sun up with a jawbone to make the days last longer.

I didn't have that kind of power. I didn't have any power at all; I could only wait for what was coming. "Say something!" I screamed.

DuPree still didn't answer. He just took that last step.

CHAPTER FOUR

"Hold on one minute," said a girl's voice. Not Susan's. It came from the shadows in the home-team dugout. "This doesn't look like a fair fight to me."

"Mario DuPree, you make it too easy," a boy's voice echoed from the visitor's dugout. "Standing all tall like that in between your two round buddies. If you shaved your head, I'd swear you were doing it on purpose."

The three of them stopped moving. DuPree's head darted sharply from left to right, like a bird's. He looked confused, but angry at the same time. It was like he had two brains in his head, fighting over what to feel.

A tall girl stepped out of the home dugout. She wore red-and-white Ponderosa Wrestling warm-ups and had blonde hair in a tight ponytail. Sage Kaiser, the wrestler from my team. She walked easily, with the confidence of somebody coming into a party where she knew everyone.

CHAPTER FOUR

DuPree and his gang were huge and violent. Sage should have been afraid. Instead she looked annoyed. "Really?" she called out. "You pull that now? How are we supposed to make a dramatic entrance with you acting juvenile all the time?"

Out of the visitors' dugout came a short, slender boy about my age. He was black, wore black and had black hair in a short afro. He walked with a thin cane in one hand. I didn't know his name, but I'd seen him sometimes in the halls.

"*Gi,*" he said, "we're 16 years old. We *are* juveniles."

"What is this?" DuPree demanded. His voice sounded weird, the way it does after you've been to the dentist and forget how to use your mouth for a while.

"This, my friend, is an intervention," said the boy with the cane. He twirled it once in his hand. "We're afraid you're about to get yourself hurt."

The three larger boys hesitated, but they didn't pull back. They looked from me, to Sage, to the little one. Their shoulders jerked and twitched like the limbs of a marionette.

"Um, Sage?" I whispered. My throat was too tight and dry for anything else. "What's going on?"

"Not now, Morgan."

DuPree's body snapped fully upright. His eyes gleamed. They looked completely black in the surrounding shadows. His head bobbed back and forth with a pecking motion. He raised his talon hands and charged straight at me.

I tensed for the impact, but it never came. Sage glided in from the side and hit him six or seven times in a quick combination of punches and chops. She rotated to follow his motion even as he stumbled from the attack and fell to his knees. Behind DuPree, Sage's partner flipped his cane across Arturo's shins, then leapt sideways and hit Ivan behind the knees. He whacked them both, across the backs of their necks with one bouncing motion each. They fell to their faces, groaning.

The much smaller boy stood over them, watching as they squirmed in the sand like little kids trying to wake up after staying awake way too late. He shouted, "Let them go!" slamming the butt of his cane into the ground for emphasis.

Sage shoved DuPree to the ground with a pushing kick to his shoulder. He hit the ground with a meaty thump and didn't move. She stood above him with a stance that said she was more than ready to kick him again. "Let him go!" Her voice had a power in it, like a bass note supporting a guitar riff. When I noticed it in her, I realized her partner's voice had the same power when he'd spoken.

All three of the thugs' bodies spasmed, and then something weird happened.

CHAPTER FIVE

As DuPree, Arturo and Ivan lay on the ground, shadows started dripping out of their ears. It looked like oil leaking out, only flowing away from the ground instead of toward it. On top of DuPree, the shadow congealed into the form of a short … thing. A short thing with a human body, but covered with feathers and sporting a crow's beaked head. The shadow above Arturo looked like one of the ghosts from an old Pac Man video game. Ivan's was a badger with six legs and a wide tail.

Beneath the shadows, the boys' bodies went limp. Long, slow breaths whistled through their mouths. Ivan started to snore.

The shadows crouched over the boys without really standing on them. They hunched and turned, trying to look at all three of us at the same time. I was so afraid I couldn't move, literally paralyzed with fear. Not even my stomach butterflies could make themselves flutter.

The badger shadow screamed in a high, wheezing cackle. It leaped into the air, straight at Sage. Something bright flashed through the air and the monster dissipated into the surrounding night. Sage's partner stood in a wide stance, sliding a thin blade back into his cane. The other shadows scuttled away and over the fence, moving in low, impossibly long leaps.

"Yeah! That's right!" Sage's partner shouted after them. His voice echoed against the brick walls of our high school. "You'd better run! Hey, you kids! Get off my lawn!"

DuPree and the others still lay on the ground, leaving me alone with Sage and the Last Samurai. My legs gave up on me. I slid to the ground, my bare back scraping painfully along the cold, rough metal of the chain-link backstop.

My rescuers bowed to one another. Not deep bows, just little nods of their heads. They turned and started walking out of the baseball diamond.

"Um, guys?" My voice was still just a whisper. They didn't respond.

I cleared my throat and swallowed to get some moisture. I said it again, not shouting, but louder. Neither of them turned around, but they seemed to slow just a little.

"Um, thanks and all," I said, "but just what the heck is going on?"

"We'd tell you ..." the little swordsman called over one shoulder. He was still walking away.

"But then they'd try to kill you," said Sage.

"Again," said her partner.

And then they were gone.

CHAPTER SIX

Cold seeped into my shoulders from the metal backstop and into my rear from the sand below me. Puffs of vapor drifted up from the mouths and noses of the three guys lying unconscious in front of me. My mind spun. Had I really seen what I thought I saw?

There had to be some kind of mistake, maybe a mental episode. That guy from Washington had nearly choked me out, and then DuPree scared me out of my scull. I wasn't thinking clearly, had to pull myself together. Things would make sense if I could just focus.

Most of all, though, I had to move. If I sat there long enough, I could literally freeze to death. It's hard to die of hypothermia in Portland, Oregon, but sitting still on the ground in your underwear, in January, at night is a great way to try. If I didn't die, a janitor or school safety officer might come along eventually. The situation would be hard to explain, even to a war hero who thought I was all right.

I pushed through foggy thoughts and stiffening muscles and made myself stand up no matter how much my body wanted to stay put. As the adrenaline faded from my system, I wished I couldn't feel my toes at all. My feet had reached that extra-special kind of cold where they weren't numb yet and touching anything at all hurt. Walking back through the grass would only make them wet. I didn't want to do that, but anything that came from staying here would be worse. Probably much worse.

"Adios, my friends," I said to the sleeping trio. It sounded braver than I felt. I looked them over as I walked past. They'd be all right, fully dressed and wearing winter coats. DuPree looked so normal, even small, lying there in his open letterman's jacket. As normal as somebody can look when he's unconscious in a high school baseball field.

Unless all four of us had shared some kind of drug, that scene a moment earlier had been real. And there was no way I'd done any drugs. Thank my dad's example for that. What the heck was going on? My mind flailed around for a rational explanation even as I moved past DuPree and back toward the school.

Winter dew and clipped grass clung to my feet as I hop-ran through the field. It hurt even worse than I'd thought it would, but not nearly as bad as the concrete path around the school did. So much colder than the grass, the concrete seemed to freeze the water on my feet into sandals made of ice. I ran across the walk, wincing and saying "ouch!" with every step, heading for the door I'd run through earlier.

Inside would be warm. I could get into my clothes, put on my socks and shoes. I could even take another hot shower if they didn't turn the water off at night. Susan would have to be long gone by now, hopefully forgetting I ever existed.

I hurried to the door and pulled the handle. It was cold against the bare skin of my hand. Cold and locked.

Locked. Like school doors are at night. Locked and between me and my clothes. Between me and my shoes. Between me and my cell phone. Between me and my wallet and the keys to my bike lock.

I said a very, very rude word.

I hopped from one foot to the other, using that word with every stinging, tingling slap of my sole on the pavement. My breath came out in puffy white clouds as I snarled each filthy syllable.

A light flashed to my left: headlamps in the student parking lot. I didn't even think, just ran toward the car as fast as my numbing feet would let me. The staff lot would have been better, with a teacher or some other adult with keys to the school, but a student might at least give me a ride home. I could go inside and get dressed, except I didn't have my keys. Maybe whoever it was would wait with me, let me stay in a heated car until mom got home. It couldn't be that long before midnight. Heck, sitting in a car mostly naked with a random stranger wouldn't even be the weirdest thing I'd done that night.

The car started moving. I kicked myself into overdrive, forcing my feet across the asphalt toward the sweeping headlights, screaming a little when my feet hit the ground after I hurdled two divider strips.

Details came into view as I neared the car, an older Ford Taurus. Nothing fancy, just something to drive to school and back. That was a good sign. People who drove cars that would look right in my neighborhood usually had a higher tolerance for the unexpected.

It slowed at a speed bump. I leapt forward into the white pool of headlights and slapped the hood with both hands. The impact sent shocks of pain tingling all the way up to my shoulders. Brakes chirped as the car stopped. Through the glare of the headlights, I could barely make out the driver's bright yellow T-shirt, with a white face above it. Light brown hair fell out the back of a ball cap. It was Susan Parker.

Susan Freaking Parker.

I said that rude word again.

CHAPTER SEVEN

Susan rolled down her window. She stuck her head out as far as she could without taking her seatbelt off. Her whole face was wrinkled in surprise and confusion.

"All right, Connor Morgan. This is getting ridiculous." Her voice sounded amused and curious, not angry like the words would make you expect.

"Can I ... um?" My voice failed me. The combination of nerves, cold and a flooding embarrassment shut down my brain. I just stood in the road with my hands hanging by my sides.

"You're turning blue out there. Get in before you freeze to death."

"Really?" was all I could push through my cold-swollen tongue and chattering teeth.

"Really. Get in here before your brain freezes and you turn into the epic dumb jock everybody tells me you are."

"Th-thank you."

I got in. Susan slipped the gear shift into reverse, and backed into a parking space. The lot was empty except for her car. We were alone. Together, alone, with me in my underpants. I peeked at her out of the corner of my eye. She was still smiling, the way someone does when she's just heard a joke she doesn't quite understand.

"Thank you," I said again. The heater vent blew wonderful, warm air all over my toes and legs. I rubbed my fingers together in the flow. Now that I was sitting still, I could feel just how bad I'd gotten outside. I shivered even harder.

"You're welcome," said Susan. "Now, suppose you tell me what's going on?"

I wanted to, but my brain hadn't rebooted yet. I could only focus on how great the warmth was, and how silly I felt sitting there in my skivvies.

Susan answered for me, which was a relief. If I told her what I'd seen, she'd drive me straight to the loony bin. If they still had loony bins. If not, she'd drive me straight to the police.

"This has something to do with that creep DuPree," she said. "They weren't chasing you for fun."

"No," I said. My voice was mostly steady. "But I got away."

"Ooookaaaay," she dragged the word out into twenty or so syllables. "I'm with you so far. They chased. You ran. You were faster."

I nodded. That was simplifying things, but close enough to the truth without my having to mention demon shadows or how one of our classmates might be Batman. Batwoman. Whatever.

"And now they're gone."

I nodded again. Asleep was the next best thing to gone.

"There's one part I'm not getting, though."

I winced. Maybe she had seen something. I didn't know how I could explain any of it without making things worse. If they could get worse. My voice felt tight and strained when I answered with a squeaky, "What?"

"Why is it, exactly, that you're still mostly naked?"

I could have cried with relief. The answer to that question wouldn't even make me sound crazy. Stupid maybe, but not crazy. "The school's locked."

Susan sat very still for what felt like a long time, like somebody trying to keep a bad temper under control. I held my breath. Maybe she knew more than she let on and was mad at me for lying about it.

"Ohyoupoordearthing," she said at last, all in one quick exhale. She didn't sound angry or even sympathetic. She sounded like somebody struggling not to laugh.

I blushed even hotter than I was already all the way to the tips of my thawing toes. "So," I said, "if you could, maybe, um. Could you drive me home? I have other clothes there. I can come back in the morning for my stuff before somebody takes off with it."

"I'll do you one better, Connor Morgan." Susan reached into her purse and pulled out a pink cell phone. It had one of those dangly ornaments on it, a tiny plastic statue of a hand. She dialed a number using speed dial. A girl's voice, about our age, answered. I couldn't make out the exact words, but it sounded like a greeting.

Susan said, "Tash, this is Parker. You still working?"

Pause.

"Could you come let me in? Yeah, the doors by the gym."

Pause.

"No, the wrestling gym. Not the big one."

The other voice came over loud, but not distinct enough for me to understand. It sounded like a question.

Susan said, "Oddly, closer than you might think. But no, not so much."

Another pause.

"You'll see when you get down here. Mmmkaythanksbyenow."

She hung up and said to me, "Tasha's captain of the debate team. She's always here until midnight or later working on cases and stuff. Are you ready to take a walk?"

I stifled a groan. Unless I was misinterpreting things, I was about to meet one of Susan's friends while standing in just my underwear. Maybe freezing to death hadn't been such a bad plan after all. Susan got out of her car, and all I could do was follow. My stomach did flip flops; the butterfly colony in there was now warm enough to put in their opinion. We reached the door.

Through the window, I could see a short blonde girl in loose black clothes and high black heels walking our way. She opened the door by stretching up on her tiptoes and pushing the bar latch with her rear, and then looked at us with her eyebrows raised. One of them was pierced with a narrow, silver ring. The girl, who I guessed was Tasha, stepped aside to let us in, holding the door open with her back.

"Thanks," I mumbled. A braver, cooler guy would have stopped to chat and would have said just the right thing to turn the embarrassing moment into a funny story. Like that little swordsman, *Yuuki,* had done in the ball field. Me, I just walked as fast as I could to the locker room.

Behind me, Tasha said, "My oh my, Parker. He ain't half ripped, is he?"

"I know, right?" said Susan.

"And when he blushes, it goes all the way down. I mean, look!" I tried to move faster without looking like I was hurrying. So much for white girls never noticing that.

The door swung shut and blocked out the rest of that conversation. I collected my things from the bench where I'd left them and got dressed. My socks felt amazing as I pulled the warm cotton over my toes. I'd never truly appreciated that article of clothing before. I used the mirror at the end of the aisle and did breathing exercises until the blush faded from my face. I looked like hell and hoped Susan had just gone up to the debate room with her friend Tasha, but with my luck tonight that wasn't a real possibility.

I made myself walk through the locker room door no matter how embarrassing the next few moments might turn out to be. Susan had been kind to me. If there were music to face, I'd face it for her. Besides, she had kind of said she thought I was ripped.

Susan Freaking Parker thought I was ripped. It was almost enough to make me smile.

She and Tasha were leaning together against the wall

in the same place Susan had dropped her Coke earlier. When I came through the door, they both straightened up and tried to quit laughing. Tasha had a laugh like a horse's whinny, high and loud and echoing in the empty hall. Susan hit her backhanded across the chest as she spotted me.

It must be nice having friends like that, I thought, *having more than one person to joke around with and count on when you're in a jam.*

Tasha pushed herself off the wall and started back the way she had come, waving good-bye by wiggling all five fingers of one hand. "You two kids be good now." She looked me over for a second, and added "Nice ink, stud."

That confused me until I remembered she'd seen my back while I was walking to the locker room. My birthmark must have looked more like a tattoo than I thought.

"It's not a ..." I started, then gave up. "Thanks. I like it, too."

I turned to Susan, afraid she could see me blushing again. We faced each other, not quite making eye contact.

I said, "Um, thanks, Susan. Thanks again."

"No problem." Her voice seemed relaxed, but had something beneath it, like maybe she was a little nervous herself. "Do you need a ride home?"

"I've got my bike."

"Long ride?"

"No big deal. Two miles. Mom should be home when I get there." I offered to walk her to her car and she accepted. She bumped me lightly on the arm as we walked.

"Tell me about you, Connor," she said.

"Like what?"

"Well, if this was DesperateDatingDotCom, you'd be all, 'I'm Connor Morgan. I like puppies, wrestling and long walks in the cold with no clothes on.'"

"That's all there is to tell. Tell me about you," I said.

"Nuh uh. You first."

"I've already heard my story lots of times," I insisted. "I want to hear yours."

"No way."

"Okay, okay. I'll go."

"Good," she said.

"I'm Susan Parker," I said. I made my voice higher and softer, not making fun of how she talked but sounding a bit more like a girl. "I run track in the spring and cross-country in the fall. I like stretchy pants even when I'm not working out, and I eat terrible school food for lunch. My favorite sweatshirt is from a track meet three years ago. I'm mostly a happy person, but every once in a while I look sad when I get to school – but I usually cheer up by lunchtime."

Susan stopped walking. She stared at me with her eyes wide and maybe a little damp. "I, uh … Connor … that's, well, that's either really sweet or kind of creepy."

"Do I get a vote?" *Idiot,* my mind shouted at my mouth, *you went too far. You've scared her off.*

But she didn't run away. Instead she said, "How did you know it's my favorite sweatshirt?"

"All your other clothes are new and nice. That one's faded, too small for you, and has a tear in one sleeve that looks like you sewed it up yourself."

"Wow," she said. "You've been paying attention."

"Well, to you. A little. Now and then," I rasped. I tried to clear my throat, but talking and breathing were suddenly trickier than usual.

"Okay then," Susan said. We walked the last few steps to her car. "Listen here, Connor Morgan."

"Yeah, Susan Parker?"

"I've already gotten farther with you tonight than I was going to let you get with me. Lots farther."

I stared. My mouth might have fallen open, just a little.

"So … I think I'm going to say good night."

"Okay," my mouth said. My brain was still working through that earlier sentence.

"See you in class tomorrow?"

"Sure," I said. "Yeah. I mean, yes. Absolutely, yes."

Susan put one hand on my arm. I could feel its warmth even through my winter jacket. She leaned up on her tip toes and kissed me once, gently, on the cheek.

"All right then, Connor. Tomorrow."

"Yeah," I whispered. "Tomorrow." I watched her open her car door and slide in. She shut the door, started the engine and waved as she drove away and out of sight. I waved back.

Susan Freaking Parker. I could still feel the kiss, a tiny warm circle on the cold surface of my cheek. Suddenly, tomorrow didn't look half bad.

CHAPTER EIGHT

Rain poured on me the whole ride to school, and the bad traffic that always happens in Portland rain made me late so I couldn't see Susan before class. Mrs. Kellar gave us a pop quiz in Psychology, which I worked hard on and maybe got a C. It took the whole class for me to finish, so I didn't get a chance to do more than look at Susan. For dessert, Mrs. Kellar dropped a three-megaton homework bomb on us all — a five-page essay on psychology and war. Due Monday, first thing.

The rest of the day went about that well.

Between classes, Susan spent every second of every passing period surrounded by her friends. Whenever I came close, they all looked at me. I just knew every single one had heard about the night before, at least the parts that were most likely to make them giggle in that tone. No way was I ready to talk with Susan so outnumbered. I never even found a minute to get her phone number or email. Not even her Facebook handle or Instagram name.

As if that weren't enough aggravation, I kept spotting *Yuuki* in the hall. Sometimes he had his cane with him. Other times he didn't. I wanted to catch up and ask about what happened on the ball field. It seemed like he took things less seriously than Sage, so he'd be more likely to let something slip. Every time I saw him, he vanished into the crowd before I could say hello.

It was just that kind of day, but walking into the wrestling room fixed a lot of it. Most high schools have one, a smaller gym space tucked into the back corner of the athletics wing like the teachers are ashamed it's there at all. Sometimes I think a lot of teachers disapprove of something so physical being part of their academic world. But it's part of high school culture, so they have to let us barbarians keep our little space.

Much as some teachers might not like it, you can tell in any good wrestling room that the coach and athletes are proud. The room is usually clean with well-scrubbed mats on the floor and along the bottom half of the walls. Ponderosa's mats were red and white to match the school colors. Every single room I ever worked out in had art on the walls. Most teams get a painter or a sketch artist on the squad at one time or another, and the walls end up covered with action images, inspiring quotes and a wall full of medals.

Different schools do the medals differently. It might be a line of actual medals, or paintings of medals or little metal plaques, but they're always there. The name, weight class and accomplishments of every wrestler who took a major title in the history of that program are up there forever, for everyone to see.

Ponderosa used names, weights and years painted inside a circle the color of the medal that the athlete won. Gold for first, silver for second, bronze for third. One year — maybe this year, but probably next — my name would decorate a wall. In gold, if I had anything to say about it.

My name would be there forever. No matter where I went, no matter how many times my dad's violence made us move, no matter what happened to me, it would be there. Permanently. Kids who'd never met me would know my name and what I'd done. Maybe not at Ponderosa, but at whatever school I was wrestling for when I made it happen.

In a room like that, you can't help but feel powerful and ready for the workout you're about to grind your way through. Which means you feel ready for anything. Like Dan Gable, the legendary coach at University of Iowa, says, "Once you have wrestled, everything else in life is easy."

Just walking in made me stand straighter. The weight of the day lifted off my shoulders, leaving me to focus on practice.

I scanned the room and saw Sage warming up with Srini in the far corner. I called to her, but she didn't seem to hear. At the sound of my voice, DuPree broke off practicing and came straight at me. Fear rolled through my belly and down my legs, but I didn't back away. Wrestling practice was my space — any wrestling practice in any school. Nobody was going to chase me out of it. Besides, the coaches were around to keep him from killing me too badly.

DuPree smiled when he came up. He did punch me, but it was in the arm. The way guys do.

"Good work last night, Morgan," he said. "That pin would have stuck me."

I blinked. This was the guy who tried to waste me less than 24 hours earlier. The guy I'd seen beaten into unconsciousness and maybe possessed by some kind of demon if I could trust what my eyes and ears had told me. And now he was shooting the breeze with me like none of that had happened.

"Thanks," I managed.

DuPree punched me again, another mostly friendly chuck on the arm. "Don't let it go to your head, *chachi.* No way would I have fallen for that roll he suckered you with. That was rookie." He trotted back to his partner and continued his warm-up.

Carlo Urquidez called me over. He was in our heavyweight wolf pack; not on the varsity, but still on the team. Carlo isn't much of a challenge, but he's fun and knows how to work hard. My head buzzed as I jogged over to him. From aggravated to calm to scared to confused in less than 60 seconds. That had to be some kind of record.

We usually switched partners every few minutes during practice to try moves against different body types and wrestling styles. If you always work with the same person, you get in trouble when a competition hands you something else. Sage managed to be on the other side of the mat whenever we swapped. I usually rolled with her a few times every day, but never got anywhere near her that practice. She was gone by the time I got changed and out of the locker room. I rode home through the rain with no more answers than I'd had riding in that morning.

CHAPTER NINE

Mom sighed and put her spoon down in the bowl. She'd only eaten two bites of the peanut soup we'd made. "Honey," she said, "I have to cancel on bad-movie-and-good-pizza night tomorrow."

On top of the steaming brown pile of day I'd had so far, Mom's news was disappointing, but no surprise. At least I'd have time to defuse that homework bomb Mrs. Kellar had dropped on us.

"Well, rats," I said. I tried to keep my voice cheery and to smile with at least my mouth. I was disappointed, but letting Mom know that wouldn't change whatever was taking her away. It would just make her feel worse about it than she already did. "I was looking forward to watching you cry at some flick that's older than I am. Did you get called in?"

"Worse," she said. She reached across the table and touched my hand with her fingers. Her elbow bumped our salt shaker and it fell over. "They arrested your father again. The district attorney wants me to go down to Eugene and testify at his sentencing."

I looked at Mom's hand, at the tiny scars in her wrist from where they'd inserted the pins after that time my dad came after me with a tennis racket. It happened when I was nine, and Mom's broken arm had probably saved my life. That was after the second move, when my dad's therapist and Narcotics Anonymous sponsor both said he'd gotten himself together.

"I'll drive down Saturday and spend Sunday going over testimony with the prosecutor. They say with his history, your father can go away for a long time. Maybe long enough to make some actual changes. I'll sleep at Gran's house, testify early Monday morning and drive home straight after."

I righted the shaker. My fingers swept the spilt salt into a neat pile of white granules, almost like they were doing it on their own.

"What did he do this time?"

"Oh, honey," Mom let the words out in a long, sighing breath. "What doesn't he do?"

"Okay. What was he *caught* doing this time?"

"Buying meth. Or selling meth. Or stealing something so he could get some meth, or just being stupid when he was on meth. He beat up a cop when they arrested him, so he's on charges for that, too." Mom's voice was tight and angry, worse even than most of the times we talked about my dad.

"So I'll be alone for the weekend?"

Mom's face had a faraway look, and she shook her head to come back to me. "What?"

"I'll be alone?"

"Yes, honey. I'm sorry."

I grinned. "Did I mention Susan and I had kind of a moment Thursday after my match?"

"Susan Freaking Parker?" Mom asked.

"Yeah. Susan Freaking Parker. Maybe she can come over and keep me company."

Mom barked. Her laughter was all about animal noises. A snort meant amusement. Barks were more like sarcasm. "Over my dead body. Mrs. D. will check on you to make sure you're all right."

Mrs. D. — Mrs. Dochevnya — was an elderly lady who lived downstairs. She came from Ukraine or maybe Bosnia. Some tough old country like that. I helped her carry her groceries our first week in the apartments, and she had sort of adopted us. She talked with Mom a lot and ate with us once or twice every week.

"You mean she'll check to make sure I'm not too great."

Mom smiled, even though her eyes were wet in the corners. "I know you'd do the right thing without her around, but I'm a mom. I fret. It comes with the uterus. Promise me you're okay about me breaking our date."

"Mom, I'm fine."

"But not too okay. Promise you'll miss me."

"Mom, I'm heartbroken. I'll miss you like, well, like somebody from Shakespeare missed somebody else from Shakespeare so much that something dramatic happened."

She gave one of those laugh-sobs people do sometimes and came over to hug me while I still sat in my chair.

I hugged her arms with one of mine.

"I love you, too, Mom. You working tonight?"

Mom straightened up and wiped her eyes. "Yes. Graveyard. I already have to miss Monday, so I can't afford to miss tonight."

"You start at 10, right?"

"Yeah, kiddo."

"I'll clean up. You get some rest."

She did and so did I. At 20 minutes of 10, I was brushing my teeth in the bathroom mirror. Mom passed the doorway, wearing her winter coat over blue scrubs and those funny plastic sandals medical people wear.

"Save some lives, Ma!" I shouted around my brush and suds. She air-kissed at me, shut the door and locked me in from the outside.

I walked into my bedroom and past my wall of posters. No matter where Mom and I lived, I always had three posters where I could see them from where I slept. One was of Coach Dan Gable, wearing a tie and looking intense. Another showed Cael Sanderson, Olympic gold medalist and the only wrestler to ever go undefeated for an entire NCAA wrestling career. The third was of Kyle Maynard, a guy who wrestled competitively in high school despite having no arms or legs. His book *No Excuses* was one of the few I'd read more than once. Even when Mom and I had to share a studio apartment, those guys were up on that wall. It was part of how I knew a space was mine, no matter how small or temporary or scary that space might be. For me, Mom and those posters were home. Wherever home happened to be.

I sat on my bed and shucked my shoes off. "Well, guys," I said, "it's been a weird week."

Coach Gable said, You've had harder.

Cael Sanderson looked down from his poster, headgear dangling from one hand. He said, *H*arder, but not weirder.

I want to make it very clear that the posters did not actually talk to me. That's like something out of a book for kids. Nor did I believe they were really speaking to me. I'm not crazy. It was more like I imagined what I thought these guys — my heroes, the men I wanted to be like as an adult — would say if we had a conversation. It's something I do sometimes when I feel confused or sad or need to talk.

What can I say? I love my mom and I value her advice, but sometimes a guy just needs to talk with other guys. My dad's not an option, and my uncles live a long way away. So I talk with these guys instead.

"I know," I said. "What was that last night? There's what I thought I saw, but then there's what I know can be true."

Kyle said, How often do you hallucinate?

"Never, that I know of."

But you did get choked pretty hard, said Coach. It wouldn't be the first time oxygen deprivation scrambled an athlete's brain.

What does your gut tell you? asked Cael.

"My gut is about as confused as the rest of me," I admitted.

Then the question isn't relevant, said Gable. If it doesn't help you meet your goals, don't give it any energy.

Put it away for now, at least until new information gives you something useful to do with it.

Always the coach with that guy, muttered Kyle. His poster was a close-up of his face and torso; it's the same one that's on the jacket of his book.

But he has a point, said Cael.

When in doubt, trust your senses, Coach Gable said. Don't worry about stuff you can't know.

"So I'm not crazy?" I asked.

I wouldn't say that, Maynard said. You *are* talking to posters.

"Shut up," I said. Even my imaginary friends are wise guys. "I need some sleep."

CHAPTER TEN

My computer went "bploink."

I was multitasking, rotating between my Facebook account, researching the Enigma project for Mrs. Kellar and watching *Vision Quest* on Netflix. It's easier than it sounds. This was only my hundredth or so time watching the movie, and my Facebook conversations are usually limited to stuff like:

RandomGuyIKindofKnow: Dude, 'sup?

Me: Nothing. You?

RandomGuyIKindofKnow: Just pwning n000bs. ROFLMAO.

RandomGuyIKindofKnow is no longer online.

When you move a lot, you end up with about a gajillion Facebook friends but nobody who really gets close. It happens even when you move in secret so your dad can't find you. We'd done that twice now, and my dad only found us the first time. Stalkers are cute in the movies. They do things like impersonate strangers to get to know you or play love songs in your driveway.

In real life, they break in and wreck stuff. They steal your mom's things and sell them for drugs. They break bones and slap you so hard you see double for a week. They are scary and terrible. They're also expensive since you don't get your deposit back on apartments when you run out in the middle of the lease. My dad hadn't come for us since we moved to Portland. That was two months ago, but you wouldn't know it from how often Mom checks the door locks or from the sour feeling my stomach always gets when I saw a big Polynesian guy at a distance. There aren't that many of us in Oregon, so my gut assumes it's my dad even when there's no way it could be him.

Between the weak Facebook chats and my having memorized the movie, I was actually making progress on my report. Enigma was how the allies used math and psychology to break German codes during World War II. It saved lives. Lots of lives. I figured it counted toward Mrs. Kellar's assignment.

When my computer "bploinked," a new message box came up. It was a friend request from a name I didn't know, but I could guess who it was. A chat box appeared only a second after I accepted.

PdxSusan: You're doing this all wrong, Morgan. _You're_ supposed to stalk _me_.

I smiled. I might have shouted "Woot!" out loud in our empty apartment, but you'll never make me admit it. Talking online is easy, even talking to Susan. Sure, my hands shook on the keys and my breath came a little fast, but I could still check what I typed before sending it. You can't hit the delete key face-to-face.

Me: I tried to talk with you all day yesterday.

PdxSusan: I know, right? I saw you. It was cute.

Me: SRSLY?

PdxSusan: SRSLY. You're sweet.

My heart stopped beating for a second, then came back online hammering like the drummer from Five Finger Death Punch. Susan Freaking Parker had just called me cute and sweet. And the other night, she'd said I was ripped. Things might be going better than I'd hoped.

Me: You're sweet, too.

PdxSusan: How?

Me: What?

PdxSusan: Tell me more nice things about me. How, exactly, am I sweet?

My phone rang. I glanced to where it lay on the table to see if it was Mom or Mrs. Dochevnya. I didn't recognize the number so I hit "Ignore" and got back to the screen.

Me: It was sweet of you to let me sit in your car and get warm.

PdxSusan: You didn't leave me much choice. I couldn't abandon anybody in such a pitiful situation.

Me: So you're saying I'm not special?

I deleted and retyped that three times before sending. Maybe I was being too bold, but Susan seemed pretty clear about what she wanted.

PdxSusan is typing, the screen said. For a long time. That meant she was typing a long message or that she kept deleting and retyping just like I had. Either way, it was a good sign.

My phone rang again. The same number. I hit "Ignore." It rang again immediately. More ringing for me, more ignore for whomever was calling. Whomever it was could wait.

PdxSusan: I'm not saying you're _not_ special.

Me: Thanks. Thanks so much. Quit with the compliments before you embarrass me.

PdxSusan: What did you expect, a poem?

Me: Yes. A sonnet, like from Shakespeare.

PdxSusan: How about a dirty limerick?

Me: LOL

PdxSusan: Really?

Me: Well, kind of.

PdxSusan: I don't think I've ever seen you laugh.

More typing and deleting on my side. "That's because you make me nervous." No way — too much, too soon. Delete. "Only my mom can make me laugh." You have to be kidding me. Delete. I went for halfway inviting, halfway accusing.

Me: Only because you're not around me much.

My phone blew up with text messages. Three in a row, with pictures. They were all from that same strange number. It wasn't the number for the pizza guy, so it had to be a prank. If I opened one, I'd probably wind up staring at DuPree's junk or something. I was about ready to turn off the phone completely. I did flip it to vibrate so it wouldn't break any more of my concentration. The computer bploinked again.

PdxSusan: Well, maybe we should do something about that.

Wow, I thought. *Susan Freaking Parker. Wow.*

Me: I think so too.

PdxSusan: When are you free?

"Tonight," I wanted to say. "Tonight I'm free. I'm free and my mom's not home." But I didn't. I don't know if I was more afraid of disappointing Mom or of getting caught by Mrs. Dochevnya or of what might happen if Susan said yes.

Me: IDK. When are you free?

PdxSusan: How about tomorrow? Afternoon?

Somebody knocked on my door. It was probably the pizza guy. I got up and fished some bills out of a drawer where Mom had left some money for me to use while she was gone.

Me: AFK. BRB.

PdxSusan: :-(

My phone buzzed on the desk, rattling around among the pencils and notes. I'd spent the whole day alone, and now everybody wanted to talk to me all at once. I snatched the phone up and punched "Answer."

"What?" I shouted into the mouthpiece. "Who is this? What is so important?"

Sage Kaiser's voice came through the speaker. "Don't answer the door."

"Don't, who the huh?" The voice and her words threw a wrench into the engine of my brain. "What's going on?"

"No time. Go to your bedroom window. Do it now. Don't ask questions."

Knock, knock, knock on my apartment door. The pizza guy was getting impatient. I knew from a job my dad had for about a week that long waits cost them money. They work for tips, mostly.

"No questions. You're in danger. Move now."

With a last glance at the blinking cursor of my chat box, I decided to trust the girl who'd saved my life once already that week. I slipped through the hall into my bedroom, shut the door behind me and flipped the little privacy lock. Those locks don't do any good against a determined adult — my dad taught me that — but it helped me feel a little safer. I walked to my window and pushed back the curtain.

Our apartment was on the second floor. Below me, on a thin strip of grass between the building and the parking lot, stood Sage. A cell phone glowed in her hand, and she was staring at my window. Beside her stood *Yuuki*. No, two *Yuuki*s, side by side. Only one of them held a cane. He was dressed all in black, like he was the other night. The other wore a tropical shirt and tan shorts, even in the chilly Portland night.

Cellphone waves move at the speed of light. Sage's voice had to travel up to a satellite, then back down to Earth before it could reach my ear. I saw her lips move a fraction of a second before the word came through my phone.

"Jump."

The pizza guy knocked again, louder this time. It sounded like he was hammering with the side of his fist instead of rapping with his knuckles. Pretty aggressive for a delivery dude.

"That's my pizza at the door."

"No," Sage said. "It isn't."

One of the *Yuuki*s fiddled with his phone. A text message came through on mine. I opened it to see a photo of my front door, time stamped two minutes before. The pizza guy was there, red insulator bag held sideways in one hand. Two other guys crouched on either side of the door. They both had ball bats, but neither carried a glove.

"What the heck is going on?" I shouted into the phone. Cold sweat broke out on my neck and forehead. Those guys weren't DuPree and his friends. I'd never seen them before. How many people could want to kill me on the same weekend? "What do I do?"

Sage's voice was intense, commanding. Not with the power I'd heard the other night, just with an unshakeable certainty that she had the best plan. She said "jump" again and somehow made it sound reasonable.

The pizza guy, or whoever he was, hit my door hard — with a shoulder, from the sound of it. I grabbed my shoes and put them on. You can't say I don't learn from my mistakes. I opened my window and punched out the screen.

Below, Sage and the *Yuuki*s made a hole for me to land. Each *Yuuki* watched opposite corners of my building.

I glanced around my room. Bedrooms hadn't always been safe places for me, and I'd had a lot of them over the years. But I was starting to get used to this one. It meant something to me. Dan, Cael and Kyle looked back from their places on the walls. None of them had any advice. I wondered if any of them ever had to deal with something like this.

I sat on the windowsill and swung my feet out over empty air. I'd jumped off higher things at the beach and landed just fine, but that was onto piles of loose sand. Not onto grass and definitely not onto the asphalt that would catch me if I missed.

Another crash came from the front of the apartment. Whatever happened when I landed, it wouldn't hurt as bad as a bat to the side of my favorite head.

I breathed in, looked Kyle in the eye. He had nothing to say. Maybe I'd end up with a story like his. The winter air tasted like cold metal in my mouth.

I jumped.

CHAPTER ELEVEN

I landed on the grass with both feet, tucked and did a shoulder roll to ride out the impact. The momentum threw me to my feet and I stumble-ran off the grass into the parking lot. My toes hit one of those concrete parking bumps and I fell to my hands and knees, ripping one leg of my jeans and giving both palms a stinging case of road rash.

Yuuki – the *Yuuki* without a cane – ran up to me and held out his hand.

"Come with me if you want to live." His voice had a tone that sounded like he was doing an impression. Some politician I'd seen on YouTube, maybe. I grabbed his hand and he hauled me to my feet. Sage ran up to us quickly but quietly. She only slowed a little as she kept going right past.

"What now?" I said. I might have screamed it, just a little.

One of the baseball bat guys came around the corner, running full-tilt in that weird puppet-gait I'd seen in DuPree the other night. He was big. Not quite as big as me, but he had that bat and he wore gang colors that said he'd fight a lot dirtier than I wanted to. He moved in a straight line, running so fast he seemed to drag the shadows along behind him.

"We run," Sage called. I didn't argue.

Yuuki, the *Yuuki* with a cane, led the way. He ran quickly despite his limp. As he hit the far corner of my building, another big guy leapt into view. The gangbanger swung his bat down at *Yuuki*'s head in a double-handed swing, the way a lumberjack chops wood.

Yuuki raised his cane in a circle and deflected the bat, guiding it around himself in an arc. The aluminum head raised sparks when it hit the concrete just to the side of *Yuuki*'s foot. The other *Yuuki*, the one in the tropical shirt, ran up and rolled between Cane *Yuuki*'s legs. In a crabwalk position, he lifted one foot and drove it straight up into the big guy's crotch. When the thug bent over from the pain, the other *Yuuki* swung his cane down on the thug's head. The crack sounded like a gunshot, and the gangbanger fell.

Cane *Yuuki* helped Tropical *Yuuki* to his feet. He said "Nice one, Fiel. Way to cut the family jewels."

"Thanks, Galhardo. That was a gem of a move you pulled, too."

"Only possible because you kicked him in the stones."

"Oh, for God's sake," Sage said as we caught up and ran past.

I looked down at the gangbanger, who was already getting to his knees. An oily black shadow, bird-shaped like the one on DuPree Thursday night, clung to his back. It was digging black claws into his back like spurs. Our attackers weren't dragging shadows with them. The shadows were driving them forward.

A shiver ran laps up and down my spine. I hadn't imagined the scene Thursday night. The shadow creatures were real, and they were forcing people to attack me.

Sage said, "Don't let them hold onto you."

Not that I'd planned to. Whatever was going on, it was pretty clear who the bad guys were.

"Keep moving!" shouted Tropical *Yuuki*, or was his name Fiel? It was just one of the many things confusing me at that moment. Between the shadows and the real-life bad guys, that mystery would have to wait. He and Cane *Yuuki*/Galhardo plunged forward and we ran as a group.

My feet felt heavy in my shoes. Fear and confusion robbed speed from every step, but I followed Sage and the *Yuukis* as fast as I could make myself go.

We rounded the front corner of my building out onto the street side. Up by my apartment door, the pizza guy spotted us. He jumped from the landing to the parking lot and stuck the landing like a gymnast, moving with an angular grace that was beautiful and creepy at the same time.

The street was empty. If anybody had called the police about the racket, they wouldn't arrive in time to help us. Two gangbangers rounded the corner we'd come from, closing the gap rapidly despite their shadowy cargo. In the parking lot, a van door opened. Three more thugs got out. They all carried weapons in their hands and shadows on their backs.

Sage shouted, "Turn at every block! *Oni* make them fast but not smart. If we take corners, they won't gain enough speed to overrun us."

Cane *Yuuki*/Galhardo grabbed a stop sign with his free hand, using it to whip himself around the corner. We all did the same. Behind us, the gangbangers had trouble changing direction. Two ran halfway across the street before they could manage to turn.

We dodged through night-deserted streets, the bad guys never far behind. We cut corners. We swung on signposts. We bounced off parked cars. Galhardo kept up despite his limp. I was starting to get tired. I'm a high school wrestler. It takes a lot of running to do that to me. And still, the shadows and their puppets were no more than a block behind us.

"Galhardo," Sage gasped from her place at the front of our pack. Her breath was labored, too, billowing out of her in the cold air like smoke from a freight train. "Where are we?"

"Too far," Galhardo gasped. "They're between us and the dojo."

"The what?" I asked. I was breathing so hard both syllables hurt like kicks to my gut.

"Not now, *Chuugi*," said Fiel, the *Yuuki* in a tropical shirt.

"That's not my name."

"Oh," Fiel panted, "but it is."

"What?"

"I promise to explain when we're not in imminent peril," Sage said.

"Can't I have just a little peril?" Galhardo panted.

"Oh, for …" Sage wheezed. She cut a hard right, squeezing into a narrow gap between two office buildings. We slipped in behind her before the chasing crowd could round the corner behind us.

Inside was an alcove for trash cans and storage. Come summer, it would be a perfect camp for a homeless person. Most went to shelters or down to California in winter, so we had it all to ourselves. I leaned over and clutched my knees, gasping in long, ripping breaths. You're not supposed to do that. It actually makes catching your breath harder, but it was that or fall down.

Fiel was still at the mouth of the alley setting something small on the ground. He ran to join us a moment later. In the dark alley, he and Galhardo looked exactly alike except for their clothes.

"We're good," Fiel said.

Galhardo took a flat oblong thing out of his pocket: a smart phone. He pushed some points on the screen and a video came up. We crowded in to look. It showed the street out front, from corner to corner, broadcast from a camera in Fiel's phone where he'd set it on the ground. We watched tiny images of Pizza Guy and the gangbangers come around the corner in their weird, skittering run.

"Nice, Fiel," Sage whispered. She punched him lightly on the leg.

"Everybody hush," Galhardo said.

We watched the gang run closer, closer still, then past our alley without slowing down. At the next corner, the lead gangbangers stopped in confusion. The ones behind crashed into them at full speed. After a short, violent tangle, they split up. Some went straight, some right, some left. Pizza Guy stayed at the corner.

Fiel let out his breath in a long whoosh. "What's the plan?"

Galhardo gasped, still catching his breath from the long run. "We … are … leaving." He tapped his phone some more and opened a map of the city. He fiddled with it for a few breaths and then waved us close. In a tight whisper he said, "We still turn at every corner. Go right, left, left, right, right, straight, left. After that it's three straight blocks to the park."

"Didn't Sage say no straight runs?" I said.

"I know," said Fiel, "but it's the only way. The dojo is across the park through a gap in the fence."

"Tough," Sage said.

"Yeah," said Fiel, "but so are we."

"Then why are we running from this fight?"

"Because, Sage, those are grown-ass adults. And we're outnumbered. Sensei says that you never fight fair unless you're standing on a mat. And only fight unfair if it's unfair in your favor."

"Plus," Galhardo whispered, "we don't know what's going on. If we're underestimating the threat, we're cooked. We'll get curb-stomped into our next lives. If we're overestimating, we might destroy all the *oni* without learning anything useful."

I crouched with them, holding very still and trying to take in everything. One minute, I'd been cyberflirting with Susan Freaking Parker. Successfully. Now I was planning small unit tactics in a filthy alley with people I hardly knew. My hands shook and my teeth wanted to chatter, and not from the cold.

Galhardo repeated his directions. "Right, left, left, right, right, straight, left. Three blocks to the park and through. Everybody got it?"

I didn't, but I wasn't about to admit it. I'd follow Sage, like I'd been doing since this whole insane episode started.

We crept up to the alley's mouth. Fiel reached with one hand and panned with his phone. Pizza guy still stood at the intersection with his back was to us. Fiel pocketed his phone then held out a fist. Galhardo bumped it, his own hand wrapped around the handle of his cane. Then came Sage. They all looked at me until I put my fist in the pile, too.

"Go," whispered Sage. Though her voice was quiet, it sounded like an order shouted across a battlefield. "Go! Go! Go!"

We went. My legs were wobbly with fatigue, but I kept up as we ran to the first intersection and rode the sign pole for a sharp right turn. Behind us, Pizza Guy howled in a chittering, animal scream that I heard in my mind, not through my ears. We'd been spotted.

The sound got my legs back into the game. Sage stayed one step ahead of me, Fiel one step behind with Galhardo right next to him. We turned left, sprinted one block, turned left again. When we hit the next intersection, we turned right and came out on the street where we'd found the alley.

Galhardo stumbled when he put his bad leg into the street. Fiel grabbed his arm and stopped the fall and got him up and running in less than a second. They'd lost maybe two steps. Sage and I slowed pace to keep us all together. We'd done okay working as a team at my apartment. There were more enemies now, which meant none of us had a chance on our own. Especially not me. This wasn't my town. I was already lost, and if I fell behind or ran ahead, I'd be lost and alone and outnumbered. I kept my feet pumping to match everybody else's pace.

We took the next right hard, rebounding off a delivery van parked in front of a corner hydrant. Fiel helped Galhardo whether he needed it or not. We'd come to our first straightaway, two full blocks. The heavy footsteps of our pursuers grew louder behind us. I didn't turn to look.

"They're gaining," said Fiel. "Should we find a place to stand?"

"No way," Galhardo said. His voice was thick with pain. "No way. We keep going."

We cut a sharp angle for the final left turn. It helped Fiel keep his balance, but the two closest gangbangers took it even faster. They closed distance with every step of the three-block sprint to the park. I crossed onto the dirt trail with three bad guys just steps behind Fiel. As we ran through the dark spaces of the park, tree branches seemed to move on their own. The shadows at their roots seemed thicker, somehow alive. The spongy ground beneath us pulled at my feet.

I followed Sage down the trail, dodging low branches and hearing the crackling mind-shouts of the gangbangers behind us. Ahead, the trail cut through a fence and led back out into the city. Sage leapt through the gap in a long, low leap with me right behind. We came out in another narrow alley, a home for stray cats and trash cans between tall apartment blocks.

Fiel came through next, then Galhardo. The moment Galhardo's back leg hit the ground, Fiel threw a full trash can into the gap, then another. Galhardo kicked a third can into the pile, and they both turned to run with me and Sage. In front of us, the alley opened onto another city street. Across the road was a business with a glass door. Light shone from inside, seeming brighter than it should have been. Two short steps led up to the stoop in front of the door. Statues of some kind of dog or lion stood on either side of the stoop.

"There," Sage panted. "The dojo. We've made it."

The mouth of the alley darkened as two figures stepped into view: Pizza Guy and a fat gangbanger with a crowbar. My legs buckled as I tried to stop running in mid-stride. I barely kept my footing in the slick muck beneath me. They'd known our goal the whole time, maybe even suckered us into the tight space. Maybe they were just faster than us. Either way, they had us trapped.

Sage stopped, sliding on the wet ground. The trash cans behind us clanked and crashed as the gangbangers fought each other like animals to fit through the blocked opening. Some snarled and snapped like dogs, while others cawed and still others fought in vicious silence.

"You had to say it," Galhardo said. He drew his sword from its cane.

Fiel whispered, "I do not like this." Three stories above us, shadows on rooftops seemed to deepen and move. The rafters crackled with their hungry, angry calls.

Sage took a fighting stance. It wasn't a wrestling stance; looked more like something from karate or kung fu. She sucked in a sharp breath through her teeth and issued a short shout of challenge. The guy with the tire iron raised his weapon in a salute. He bowed slightly to Sage, glaring at her with eyes that seemed older than the body around them, older than the city where we stood.

Sage nodded back. Tire Iron stared, waiting for the duel to commence.

Fiel kicked him in the neck.

He came out of nowhere, leaping up and rebounding off the alley wall. His heel connected with Tire Iron's throat. The thug made a choked, gurgling noise and fell over backward.

Sage sprang at Pizza Guy and hit him with a blurring series of elbows and punches. He had a chain and swung it to hit her in the arm even as he fell back and landed on his rear in the gutter. She kneed him in the face midstride as she sprinted past him and across the street, cradling her wounded arm with her opposite hand.

We followed in a tight group, Galhardo at the rear. He whipped his blade in a tight circle. The other gangbangers popped out of the alley, some worse for wear from fighting to get through from the park. Pizza Guy and Tire Iron started to move. Sage leapt up the steps and we climbed after her. The four of us barely fit on the little stoop.

The bad guys drew closer, their shadows taking on

animal shapes like at the baseball diamond Thursday night. I saw two of the crow monsters and the six-legged badger. Others took the shapes of bears, cats and things I couldn't describe but knew from my oldest nightmares. They closed in, surrounding the little stoop. I turned and took my wrestling stance. At least we had a wall to cover our backs.

But they didn't climb up; they didn't even reach for us. They stayed in the street, pacing and squirming with impatient fury. I could taste their hate in the city air, how much they wanted to hurt us, but they never touched the stairs or the stoop.

Sage rang the doorbell.

From inside, chimes rang in the chorus of a familiar song. It sounded like "Kung Fu Fighting".

Galhardo grinned, his white teeth flashing in the middle of his dark face.

"I swear to God," Sage grumbled.

One of the dog-lion statues held a gold-painted ball. For a moment, it seemed to glow with warm light, and then I saw that the pebbled glass door of the shop had swung open, spilling light into the street. In the doorway, an old man with only a few white wisps of hair stood looking at us. He smiled cheerfully beneath bright brown eyes.

"Aah, *Chuugi*. There you are," he said. He reached out and patted me once on the shoulder. "I've been waiting for you."

CHAPTER TWELVE

The old man looked over my shoulder out at the street. He was still smiling cheerfully, but the pack of monsters sprang back as if his gaze were a physical force. They fell to the ground, unconscious. The shadows gripping the men skittered away to the safety of the alley, while more oily shadows leaked from the fallen. The dark creatures roiled over one another in their panic to escape.

When they were all gone, the man stepped back to open his door wide. He beckoned us with one thin, impossibly old hand.

"Come in," he said. "Come in. Come."

Inside was a small shop with a long counter and walls covered with shelves. Except for one table in a corner, every available surface was covered with jars, pots, bags of herbs and bundles of dried plants. The place smelled of tea, dirt, and maybe of poop. But it was that good poop smell — the kind you get in a barn or dry field, not a sewer stink. Though it had seemed bright from the dark of the alley, the room was dim. The only light came

from behind a curtained doorway behind the counter.

Sage stumbled in next. She clutched her injured arm with her good hand and held her teeth tightly together. A tall, thin, pale girl about our age came through the curtain and led Sage to the table. She turned on a bright electric light and unwrapped the heavy metal chain from around Sage's forearm. Though her face was white with pain, Sage made no sound. Not even her breathing changed.

Galhardo and Fiel came in last, fast and together. They moved like two parts of the same person, the way I'd move my arm and leg in coordination to wrap somebody for a pin. Galhardo limped heavily, but moved like he was used to it. He was hurting, but he was not really injured.

"How is *Gi?*" asked the old man. He spoke with a slight accent, like with the clipped syllables I'd heard in old Japanese movies.

The tall girl spoke. Under the bright work light, she seemed paler than anybody I'd ever seen. She had pale blonde hair over a pale pink face with pale blue eyes. She said, "The skin is torn, Sensei, badly in some places, but it won't need stitches. Nothing is broken." She snapped open the wax seal on a ceramic jar, filling the shop with a smell of rose petals and rotten eggs. She smeared an orange paste over Sage's cuts.

The old man they called Sensei looked at me. "*Chuugi,*" he began.

"That's not my name."

Sensei looked at me, still with that calm, cheerful smile. He didn't say anything.

"Sir," I added. I couldn't help myself. Some people just demand that by the way it feels they're looking right into you, hoping you'll be the person you could be instead of just who you are.

"Oh?' he said. "*Chuugi* means 'loyalty' in the Nihongo, the Japanese. Your name is Connor. Connor is from the English word 'constancy,' as in a dependable and faithful friend. As in loyalty. *Chuugi* is your name, child. And so much more than the sound they use to call you."

He walked through the curtained doorway, parting a brightly painted picture of a carp. In the corner, Sage inhaled sharply, once, as the pale girl tightened down a cloth bandage.

Sensei's head popped back through a slit in the curtain. It looked like a severed head on a bright tablecloth, if severed heads could look quietly amused.

"Follow," he said. His head disappeared. I followed.

I expected the back room of a little shop, but the shop was the little back room of what I walked into.

We stood in a high-ceilinged room as big as the gym at Ponderosa High. The walls and beams were old, dark wood, and straw mats covered the floor. A few small windows sat high on the walls. Below them hung weapons like swords and spears, and not just from Asia. I saw fencing sabers, European long swords, three kinds of bow, even a modern police nightstick. On the floor, training dummies stood between bags that hung from the ceiling. A wrestling mat occupied one corner of the room, and a low boxing ring stood in the corner diagonally opposite. Next to the curtained doorway was a long, low table.

Sensei walked away. "Sit," he said over his shoulder, waving at the table. He slipped through another doorway, this one covered with a curtain bearing a picture of a coiling dragon.

Galhardo and Fiel had slipped in behind me and were already at the table. They sat on the mats, their legs folded beneath them like samurai in an old movie.

I sat down, folding my legs beneath me just like Galhardo and Fiel. They both avoided eye contact with me, staring straight forward at the middle of the table — though I thought Galhardo was trying not to grin. As we sat, I began to notice small differences between the two brothers. Fiel had wider eyes, and Galhardo's arms were thinner, less muscled.

I looked around the room. I'd been in karate schools before. Most had posters all over the walls. Inspirational posters, announcements for sales and specials, posters of rules, flyers for upcoming birthday parties or belt graduations, pictures of teachers and students. The walls here had no posters. Besides the weapons, the only decoration was a single scroll. It had to be 10 feet long and as wide as my shoulders. It looked ancient. Japanese writing covered it in a pattern that simultaneously comforted and energized me.

By the door Sensei had gone through, a set of wooden shelves reached up to waist level. The lower shelf held a collection of scrolls and books. All of them looked at least as old as the scroll on the wall.

The top shelf held seven Japanese lanterns, the stone kind you sometimes see in gardens. Each was about the size of a basketball with Japanese writing carved through the sides. The writing on each lantern was different. Three of the seven flickered with the light of a candle inside. One lit lantern's writing was a square box with a pattern of lines beneath it. Hairs stood up across the back of my neck and down both arms.

The symbol on that lantern was the same as the birthmark on my back.

A rustling noise behind me made me jump. I snapped my head around to see Sage come in, followed by the pale girl. In the brighter light of this room, I recognized her from Ponderosa. We didn't share any classes, but I'd seen her in the halls and cafeteria. She spent a lot of time near the art studios and her name started with an .A.. Allison, maybe, or Amber? Amy?

I looked up at Sage. "How's your arm?"

"Better than the *oni* who smacked it." She grimaced with pain as she sat at the table, but turned it into a ferocious grin.

"*Oni*?" I asked.

Sensei came back through the curtain carrying a wooden tray with a box, some cups and a tea pot. Steam rose gently from the spout of the pot.

"Later," Sage whispered.

Sensei walked to the table and knelt at its head. He balanced the tray perfectly as he crouched without rattling the cups or sloshing the water. He rinsed out each of the teacups with water from the pot, then opened the box and used a tiny wooden spoon to measure tea powder into each. He filled the first with a trickle of water, then the second.

My legs were falling asleep in their awkward fold. I tried not to fidget, despite the tingling in the bottoms of my feet. Sensei filled the remaining cups and passed them around, one for each of us. When we'd all been served, he lifted his own cup and sipped with a loud slurp. He set it down, smiling as he had since he opened the door.

"*Chuugi*. Please sit comfortably."

I did. My legs tingled worse as I switched to a cross-legged position, but the pain faded quickly as my blood flow returned to normal.

Sensei said, "Welcome. I imagine you have questions."

CHAPTER THIRTEEN

"Yes, sir," I said. "Yes, Sensei. I do."

"Can they wait until you've heard a story? You may find it provides some answers."

I nodded.

"Long ago, the princess Fuse-Hime was murdered, while pregnant. Her father's trusted regent killed her because he wanted the power of the throne for himself. As she died, the spirit of her baby left her body as seven green orbs. Each bore the symbol, and carried the essence, of one of the ethical principles of Bushido, the code of the warrior."

It was probably my imagination, but my shoulder blade seemed to tingle. I glanced at the lantern bearing the symbol that was on my back. Sensei went on.

"The seven orbs found seven pregnant women and merged with the life force, the *chi*, of the baby growing inside. Those babies grew into warriors of great power and courage, each a paragon of the Bushido principle that came to him in the womb. When those warriors met, they recognized each other as kin and worked together to make Japan a better place for all people.

"Wait," I said, "wasn't that a movie?" I was sure I'd seen that story on Netflix once or maybe in a comic book.

Galhardo answered. It was the first time he'd spoken since we came inside. "Yes. And a TV show and at least three video games. And plays. And cartoons. It's a popular story in Japan."

"It's a lot like the story of Robin Hood or King Arthur here in the West," said the pale girl. Even her voice was pale — thin and quiet, but still easy to hear.

"Most of the stuff you see about it today is based on a fiction series published during the 19th century," Sage added.

"Which itself was based on truth," Sensei resumed. He didn't seem upset by the interruption. A lot of adults I knew would have been. "Most legends and stories are. The trick is to discern which truth a given story tells. When the warriors died, others were born with the marks and the essence of Bushido."

"Sensei," I asked. "Bushido. You keep using that word."

Galhardo muttered, "I do not think it means what you think it means."

Sensei glanced at Galhardo, looking puzzled but not angry. He looked back to me.

"What is Bushido?" I asked.

"Bushido is the code of the warrior, the soul of the samurai. It defines who we are, how we act, how we live and how we die."

"But what is it?" I asked. I felt like I was missing something important. Everybody else at the table was sitting at straight-backed attention, like soldiers hearing the Pledge of Allegiance. The room felt quieter, more solemn, than it had a moment before.

"Bushido consists of seven ethical principles, the same principles that became a part of the Bushido Champions. Those principles are *Gi,* Duty," he nodded at Sage.

"*Yuuki,* Courage," he turned his face to Galhardo.

"*Meiyo,* Honor," he looked at Fiel.

He turned to the pale girl next, saying, "*Jin,* Compassion," then he looked at me. "*Chuugi.* Loyalty."

Sensei looked into the middle distance, toward us but not at any of us. "*Makoto* and *Rei,* Truth and Courtesy, have not yet joined us. Each of you bears a Mark of Bushido. You are the Bushido Champions of this time."

Fiel and Galhardo rolled up the short sleeves of their shirts, revealing birthmarks that looked a lot like mine. Each had a slightly different pattern from mine and from each other's. The marks were on opposite shoulders, Fiel's on the right and Galhardo's on the left. *Jin,* the pale girl, tapped her back just below her neck. A single line poked out above the collar of her shirt.

Sage sat very still, the tips of her ears bright pink. I'd seen Sage in a wrestling uniform and never spotted a birthmark of any kind. If I couldn't see hers under those conditions, she probably didn't want to talk about its location in public.

"Is it like reincarnation?" I asked.

"I confess I do not know if the soul of a Bushido Champion passes from one body to the next or if only the responsibility and power flow down the river of generations. Sometimes I see something that makes me think one way. Sometimes, I see evidence of the other. Sometimes, the mark appears on a person years after birth."

I didn't want to believe what I was hearing. Way past midnight, a total stranger was telling me about impossible things from fairy tales. Fairy tales from a country I'd only heard about in school. The last time anyone in my family had even visited Japan was when my mom's grandfather went there with the U.S. Navy. That hadn't been a social call.

Which brought a question to mind. "But Sensei, you're the only person at this table who's Japanese."

"True," Sensei said. "It seems that as ideas have spread through the world so have the Bushido Champions. They collect where they are needed and come from all countries and races."

I still didn't want to believe, but the story stirred a part of me. That part of me that sits just below my belly and right in front of my spine. The part that knows when you love somebody and that grows large during a perfect moment. That part knew Sensei told the truth. Another part of me felt the pull of this group, the Bushido Champions, and told me that I could belong with them. It made me nervous. I missed having family every day, but that just meant I had to be all the more careful about whom I chose as friends because part of me wanted that so badly. The others stayed quiet, giving me the space they sensed I needed.

Another question came to my mind. "Sensei?"

"Yes, *Chuugi*?"

"Those lanterns over there," I pointed. "The one with my symbol. It's lit."

"Yes."

"Fiel and Galhardo's symbols, they're on lanterns that aren't lit."

Sensei said nothing. He just looked at me with interest, as though I were telling him something fascinating he hadn't known before.

"The other two unlit lanterns are they the symbols for Sage and —" I looked at the pale girl.

"Alex," she said, just loud enough to be heard. *Alex*. I'd been pretty close. Beside her, Sage's blush moved down her ears and onto her face and neck.

"Yes," Sensei said. "They are for *Jin* and *Gi*."

I was almost afraid to ask the rest of my question. Being the different person in the room sometimes means you've been singled out for something good. Most of the time it means just the opposite. But this place, the dojo, it felt safe. It felt like I'd always thought a home would if you lived in it for more than a few months. My voice trembled as I asked. "Why is mine lit?"

Sensei stood. He walked, smoothly and without a word, across the grass mats of the room. When he reached the lanterns, he stopped in front of mine. He gazed at the fire for a long moment, and then took in a deep, slow breath. He blew out the candle, then returned to the table and folded himself to sit in his place.

"In certain festivals in Japan, like your Halloween, we light lanterns to attract and guide the spirits all around us. *Chuugi*, we light these lanterns to guide a warrior spirit home."

All around the table, everyone was looking at me. For the first time in my life off a wrestling mat, I was the center of attention without feeling nervous and judged. I scanned the faces of Fiel, Galhardo, Alex, Sage and Sensei. I felt welcome, cared for and safe. I felt like I had come home.

It was a perfect moment, a time when what's happening and *should be* happening are in synch. It was a beautiful moment, a solemn and important moment.

Naturally, my cell phone rang.

CHAPTER FOURTEEN

I jumped. The brothers jumped. Alex squealed. The notes of my ring tone echoed from the wooden walls of the room. I peeked down at the display. Mom, calling after midnight. I winced and mumbled, "I, um, I have to take this."

"It's his mommy," Fiel said, craning his neck to peer at my screen.

"Shhh," I said. "I'm supposed to be at home. Alone." I pushed the button. "Hello?"

"Connor Morgan!" Mom's voice exploded through the speaker. First and last name was bad. Not as bad as first-middle-last, but she was definitely in a fighting mood."

"Mom?" I said. I tried to make my voice sound concerned and surprised. "What's wrong?"

"Don't you dare ask me what's wrong. Mrs. Dochevnya just called me." Her voice was so loud Galhardo could hear every word. Even Alex, who sat farthest away, raised her eyebrows at the dangerous tone in Mom's voice.

"Why would Mrs. D. call you at 1 in the morning?"

"Oh, I don't know. Why wouldn't you be home at 1 in the morning?" Across

the table, Alex tried to hide a smile behind her hand. Galhardo rolled his eyes at Fiel.

"What do you mean, Mom?"

"What do I mean? Did you really just say to me, 'What do you mean?' Mrs. Dochevnya called me. She said there was some kind of gang fight at the apartments. She got worried. You didn't answer your door, even when she knocked loud enough to wake her husband."

"Mom, Mrs. D.'s husband's been dead for years."

"That's what I mean. When you didn't answer, she called me. I called you an hour ago. You didn't answer your phone any better than you answered the door."

Mom expanded on the theme for what felt like hours. Fiel and Galhardo flopped onto their backs, squirming with the effort to keep their laughter silent. Alex covered her mouth with both hands as her shoulders shook. Even Sage smiled.

I cut in with an occasional "Mom, I —" but she cut me off each time with another stream of angry, frightened syllables.

"Connor Iraeia Morgan, are you using drugs?" The words boomed loud enough to echo off the nearest wall.

Alex snorted through her hands, and the snort turned into a high, loud, ringing laugh. There was a silence from Mom's end. Everyone at the table held their breath. Except Sensei. He looked at me and the phone with the same cheerful smile he'd had when he opened the door and drove away a pack of demons.

My mother exploded again. "Connor Iraeia Morgan, is that a girl?"

Galhardo looked up at me, his face mournful and amused at the same time. Alex couldn't help herself, and neither could Sage. They collapsed over the table in fits of rolling laughter.

"Girls," Mom said. "Plural. Connor, explain yourself immediately."

"Yes, Mom. I can explain. It's not what you think." That much was true. It wasn't likely Mom would be thinking of anything close to what was going on. But what could I say? Not "Mom, it turns out I'm some kind of superhero with a lantern instead of a cape." That wouldn't fly even if she were in a good mood. I said, "Um."

"I. Am. Waiting." Mom said. Her voice was hard and clipped tight, like it always got when she was angry because she was afraid.

Sensei reached for my phone. I shrugged and handed it over. I couldn't imagine how he could make things worse.

"Mrs. Morgan?" he said. A disgusted snort issued from the speaker. "I apologize, ma'am. Ms. Reese."

Mom's voice was muffled, but still audible. "Who. Is. This? Why are you with my son?"

"Ma'am, my name is Tetsuo Kano. I'm family of Sage Kaiser. Your son knows her from the wrestling team."

Silence.

"Sage and Connor were outside your building when the violence began. She took him here to my house to be safe."

More silence.

"We got to talking and lost track of time. Connor is safe, and we'll run him home right away."

I could hear Mom's voice, but I couldn't make out the words. At least she'd stopped shouting.

"No, ma'am. He's perfectly fine."

More indistinct sounds through the speaker.

"No, ma'am. I'm not experienced with drugs personally, but I don't believe he's 'on' any."

More sounds.

"Yes, ma'am. All right. I apologize for a part in frightening you. I know how you must fret. You're very welcome. It's been a pleasure to meet you both. Yes, of course. Here he is."

Sensei handed me my phone.

"Connor," Mom's voice was normal, and we were back to just my first name.

"Hi, Mom."

"Why didn't you call?"

"It was late. I know you have a lot to do tomorrow. I didn't want to wake you."

"You know better than that."

"I sort of didn't think to. It's been a weird night."

"Is this uncle, this Tetsuo, weird?"

"No, Mom. He's fine. I'm fine. We're all fine."

Galhardo leaned into his brother and muttered, "How are you?"

Fiel whispered back, "It was a boring conversation anyway." Sage rolled her eyes at them while they both giggled.

"If there's a problem you can't talk about out loud," Mom said, "just say 'I know, Mom.' I'll send help."

"Sure thing. Just the opposite."

"You're sure?"

"Yes, Mom."

"And you're sure you're all right?"

"Yes. Not a scratch." How that wasn't a lie I'll never know, but I was in one piece. Not a hair out of place despite all that went on that night. Even the road rash from my jump to the pavement was no more than a red mark on each palm.

"And you'll go home? It's late."

"Yes, Mom."

"And you'll let somebody drive you. It's not safe to wander around town at this hour."

"I will, Mom."

"Okay," Mom said.

"Okay," I said back.

"Yes. Okay. Just tell your mother one more thing."

"Sure, Mom. Anything. What's up?"

"Who's Sage?" she said loud enough for the whole table to hear. Sage blushed again. Alex giggled. Fiel and Galhardo just stared.

"I love you, too, Ma. Good night, now," I said.

"I love you, son." She hung up.

Everybody started talking at once. Galhardo and Fiel picked themselves up and hugged me like a brother in arms. Alex kept shaking her head and saying "Wow" over and over again. Sage wanted to know what was with my mom and whether or not I was on drugs. Sensei clapped his hands once. We all hushed.

"Tonight's attack was unprecedented," he said. Even with the deep smile lines around his eyes and mouth, his face was grave. "They knew you, *Chuugi*. Somehow, they knew who you are even before we did. If we had been even an hour slower, your mother's fears might have been correct. This kind of coordinated attack is unusual for *oni*. They're hungry, malicious and cunning, but they are never brave. They wouldn't conceive of such an attack on their own."

"What, then?" Sage asked. Her face had changed from amused to focused.

"I fear a *yokai*."

"*Yokai*?" I asked. Galhardo and Sage said it along with me.

"An elder demon. The name means *beautiful calamity* in old Japanese. They're larger, older and more powerful than the *oni*." Alex said. "Depending on the myth you read, they're the lasting spirits of evil men and women, or they're entities that live separately from the cycle of mortal life and death. Whatever they are, they can control *oni*."

Sensei nodded approval. "They lead lesser demons like a shepherd leads a flock of sheep. A *yokai* can make *oni* powerful. It can organize them, and it will lead them all to slaughter if that suits its purpose."

"Like a boss monster," said Galhardo.

"More like the Pied Piper, only evil," said Fiel.

"Didn't the Pied Piper kidnap a whole village worth of children?" Galhardo said.

"Like the Pied Piper, only more evil?"

"Why would a ... a *yokai* ... come to Portland?" I asked.

Sensei said, "*Yokai* is a Japanese name, but the creatures aren't only from Japan. They live in all times and cultures. There are people in Portland. Demons of all kinds gain become more powerful by spreading human misery. Perhaps it wants to feed on negative energy. Perhaps it suits a deeper purpose that we don't understand. *Yokai* live for thousands of years. They are subtle and very patient."

"Why would it attack us?"

"Why wouldn't it?" said Galhardo. "We sort of exist to inconvenience creatures like that."

"So now what?" I asked. Maybe they already had a plan just a little more complex than the D-Day invasion, but I didn't know what it was. "What happens next?"

"We have to find it," Sage said. "Wherever it is. Take the fight to it. We can't stand around waiting for the next attack, and the next."

"Where?" Alex asked. "Portland's a big city."

Sensei said, "Does it feel coincidental that all five of you are students at the same high school?"

After a moment of thought, we all shook our heads.

"In the years I've taught you and your kinspeople, I have always felt that kismet puts you in the right place at the right time. It seems likely that the *yokai* is somewhere in your school, inhabiting the body of somebody there. It will only gain power as time goes on."

"Who?" I wasn't the only one who said it, but I think mine was the only voice that squeaked.

"That's another of the many, many things I don't know," Sensei said. "But it's something I would suggest you spend some energy trying to learn. For now, though, we are making liars of *Chuugi* and myself. His charming mother is right. It's very late. Alex, did you drive here?"

"Yes, Sensei."

"Can you take your brothers and sisters home,

please? Everybody must be here at two tomorrow afternoon."

"For what?" I asked.

"Practice," said Fiel.

I liked that answer. Despite the warm welcome and Sensei's comforting presence, fear and doubt still buzzed in my mind. But practice — I knew how to practice. I could do practice.

Driving home felt close to normal. The five of us crammed into a blue Subaru hatchback, girls in front and boys in the back. I watched the streets carefully so I could get back for tomorrow's training session and was surprised at how simple the route was after such a long chase. We talked about teachers and tests and music and movies — the kind of stuff you talk about when you don't know each other well enough to have a real conversation. You could almost forget we were spirit warriors tasked with ridding our school of a demon older than the British Empire.

You could *almost* forget.

Alex dropped me in front of my building. By the time I got to my room, my body realized how tired it was. I fell asleep in the middle of untying my second shoe, my window still open to the night outside.

CHAPTER FIFTEEN

When I was 11 or 12, my dad had me over for his first ever, and last ever, unsupervised overnight visitation. He and a buddy thought it would be hilarious to give me beer. I thought it was funny, too, and I liked how my dad smiled when he looked at me sipping from a coffee mug full of Pabst Blue Ribbon. It was fun, until I started to throw up. Then my dad's friend got mad about the couch, and my dad looked disappointed instead of happy and proud. It was even less fun the next morning when I had my first ever, and only ever, hangover.

The D.A.R.E. officers tell you that you don't have to use alcohol or any other drug to have a good time. That's true. They don't tell you that you don't have to use alcohol or drugs to feel terrible the next morning.

Which is also true.

I woke up with somebody pounding on my skull from the inside, only to find out it was just the front door. It might have been the fight against demonic forces, the fear and its accompanying hormones, the confusion or the late night — I didn't know. But I did know I hurt. My head ached. My

stomach twinged. My muscles groaned from soreness. My throat scratched when I swallowed and my eyes felt puffy at the edges.

I clawed my way awake like a, well, like a teenager trying to wake up after a hard night and not enough sleep. The knocking was an unending assault on my ears and brain as I staggered to the door and swung it open to find Mrs. Dochevnya standing there looking me dead in the sternum.

Mrs. Dochevnya was a small woman with a wrinkled face, sharp blue yes, bad hearing and excellent listening. She squinted up at me and said, "You are all right, strange boy?" Her accent reminded me of the Count from *Sesame Street*.

"Yes, Mrs. Dochevnya. I'm sorry I worried you. Did you speak with my mother?"

"Da, Da. Your mother. She says you ran like rabbit from the trouble."

I opened my mouth to object, but she talked over me. "Is good idea. Running rabbit is live rabbit. Is not dinner for wolves."

I smiled. "Good point, ma'am. I'm fine. I went to a friend's place in a safe neighborhood."

"Am not so anymore sure there is safe neighborhood. Only neighborhoods safer than others."

"That's probably true," I said.

"When I came with my Sergei, was not so. But I am old woman and you are young, strange boy. Do you need food?"

I knew better than to say yes. The kitchen clock said I had four hours to do five hours' worth of work on my

Enigma report and then get to the dojo for training. Mrs. D. made wonderful food full of spices and exotic meats, but even a short lunch would take all afternoon. It was a bit like visiting Grandma in Eugene, which we didn't do anymore because my dad would come if she told him.

"I really can't, Mrs. Dochevnya. Thank you, but I have too much homework."

"All right. Maybe next time you can run like rabbit to library."

"Maybe. Thanks for checking in on me, ma'am."

"My pleasure, strange boy. You are one of the good ones."

It's strange how even a little old lady can make you stand up straighter with a few kind words. "Thank you, Mrs. Dochevnya."

"Is not compliment. Is responsibility." With that, she shuffled down the landing and took the stairs one slow step at a time. She held the rail with one hand and her hickory cane with the other. I would have offered to help, but she would have refused. I closed my door and sat at our table in front of the computer.

Behind the screen saver, my Facebook page stared at me like an accusation. My chat with Susan was still there, ending in a stream of her responses.

Me: AFK. BRB.
PdxSusan: :-(
PdxSusan: Well?
PdxSusan: Connor, don't leave me in suspense.
PdxSusan: Come on, Connor.
PdxSusan: Connor?
PdxSusan: Are you naked again? j/k ☺

PdxSusan: What the heck, Connor Morgan?

PdxSusan: !?!

PdxSusan: Connor?

PdxSusan: Okay, whatever.

Great. Just when things looked like they were going well. I typed a message.

Me: So sorry. Emergency here. Cops and everything. Can I explain tomorrow?

PdxSusan is offline.

Maybe it was for the best. Things would be hard enough, balancing the demands of school, wrestling and saving the world without worrying about a dating life.

I fired up pages from Wikipedia, the Smithsonian Institute and Google to finish research on my Enigma report. If I'm interested I can work pretty well, and this was interesting stuff. The best part had less to do with conflict and killing, but it was still epic. The Allies — that's England, the U.S. and France when you're talking about Enigma — had to send troops into combat zones to plant false evidence of spies. They did that so that the Germans would think the Allies got their intelligence from spies and not because Enigma had broken the German codes. It was all about misdirection, about making an enemy believe one thing when something else is really going on. By the end of the war, Enigma had saved hundreds of thousands of lives.

I finished the report and printed it by 1:15. Five pages in two hours, fifteen minutes. A new record. I ran to my room to get changed for practice.

Don't, Cael said as I passed his picture. Don't go.

"What?" I said out loud. I don't always actually

speak when I "talk" to my posters, but his comment surprised me.

This is crazy, Cael said. Are you joining a cult?

It's not necessarily crazy, Coach Gable said.

No crazier than wrestling, said Kyle.

Word, said Coach. I don't know if the real Coach Gable would say that, but mine did. If he'd been real, he would have bumped fists with the poster of Kyle. I mean, if he'd been real and Kyle had fists to bump.

"That's a point," I said.

I see three options here, said Cael. Option one: They're crazy. Option two: You're crazy. Option three: There really is a secret shadow conspiracy where high school kids fight ancient enemies from the world's mythology. Which one of these scenarios makes the most objective sense to you?

"Option one is out," I said. "They'd all have to be the same crazy at the same time, and even if they were they couldn't make me see the stuff I know I saw last night."

Nobody had a response to that. It was a fair point. "As for option two … I don't feel crazy."

Aha! Cael shouted. That's just what a crazy person would say!

"Or a sane person," I grumbled. It's tough getting outsmarted by your imaginary friends.

Isn't this conversation proof that he isn't? said Kyle. A truly crazy person wouldn't doubt or question the situation.

I'm not so sure about that, Cael said.

"Also," I said, "if it's just me who's crazy, all the others would have to be crazy, too."

That's possible, Cael said.

But unlikely, said Coach Gable.

Which leaves option three, Kyle said. That this is real. Like Sherlock tells us, once you eliminate the impossible, whatever's left — no matter how improbable — is the truth.

"And if it's real," I said, "if I have the ability to help people, then I guess it's my job to find out how."

Fair enough, said Cael.

I slid my sweat pants over the shorts I'd worn all morning.

I hope they let you decorate your room at the mental hospital, Cael said as I was lacing up my shoes.

"Why?"

So I can tell you I told you so.

CHAPTER SIXTEEN

The storefront looked different in daylight. At night, with its lights at the end of the alley tunnel, it seemed shiny and clean. Now I could see the dust of the city, the litter in the gutters nearby. It looked like any shop in any town, with cinder-block walls painted a dirty yellow and spotted with graffiti. Nobody had tagged the lion-dog statues, but that was the only thing to mark the dojo as unusual in any way. I stood on the stoop between the two lion-dogs and knocked at the door.

Nobody answered.

I knocked again, and then waited. I peered through the pebbled glass hoping for a glimpse of light or movement inside.

Still no answer. Nothing behind the glass.

As I raised my hand to knock one more time, the door opened. Sensei's face appeared in the doorway. He looked up at me, a lot like Mrs. Dochevnya had that morning.

"Why did you knock?"

"I, um, I wanted to come in. It's time for practice, right?"

"Right, *Chuugi*," Sensei said, "but why did you knock?"

"Um," I said. I'd spent so much time confused lately you'd think I'd have gotten used to it.

"You don't knock at home. You come in." He vanished from the doorway, leaving it open for me. I followed behind, kicked off my shoes at the curtained doorway and walked onto the dojo floor. The others were there already, warming up.

Sage was hitting a training dummy, striking it over and over again as she walked around it in a circle. Her hands moved so fast I couldn't really see them. There was just a blur of motion. The dummy shook and shuddered as she kept up the attack. Not too far away from her, Galhardo practiced something I recognized as a *kata* – a formal dance martial artists use in practice. It involved his cane, which he whipped in tight arcs around his whole body. In the boxing ring, Fiel and Alex sparred with playful intensity. Fiel moved all over the place, springing into high jumps and gymnastic flips. His feet shot out again and again at Alex's face and body. Sometimes he'd hit her, but only hard enough to make contact. Alex seemed almost still by comparison. She moved simply and easily at the center of the kinetic hurricane that was Fiel. She moved low to the ground, swinging fluidly like her hips were made of Jell-O. For every tap Fiel gave her, Alex landed two or more pushing slaps that threw Fiel against the ropes. Both smiled every time either took a hit.

I went to the wrestling mat and started to practice drills in the air, moving my body like a real opponent was there with me. I'd been working for only a few minutes — long enough to break a sweat but not get tired — when Sensei walked onto the deck. He wore a bright-white karate uniform with a white belt tied around his waist. Although the belt was clean, it was worn and frayed with strings hanging down from the ends. Sensei strode to the front of the room next to the shelf with the books and lanterns. He reached out to a small metal bowl and rubbed its rim with a padded stick. It rang like a bell.

The others stopped in mid-motion and ran to line up in front of Sensei. I followed. They didn't seem to care what order they were in, so I slipped between Sage and Fiel. Galhardo stood to Fiel's right with Alex on his opposite side.

Sensei bowed once to us, slowly at the waist, with his palms flat together in front of his chest. We bowed back, and everybody turned to the lanterns. Still bowing, everybody spoke in the slow cadence of a pledge or prayer.

"Gi, Yuuki, Jin, Rei, Makoto, Meiyo, Chuugi."

I had just enough time to realize the last word in the chant was Sensei's name for me, but everybody stood back up before I could think about what that might mean. Sensei turned to face us.

"*Yuuki,* I believe it's your turn. I trust you have something interesting prepared."

"*Sim,* Sensei," Galhardo said. Everybody moved to form a circle around him. "We'll do something from Aikido today. Everybody here knows what that is, right?"

Everyone else nodded. I did, too, even though I really only knew it was a kind of martial art, like I knew chicken was a kind of meat. What made it different from karate or kung fu, I had no idea.

"Aikido motions come first from battlefield sword techniques. Watch." Galhardo tucked his cane into the belt of his uniform then drew the sword blade out in a long, sweeping cut. He shuffled slightly then sliced down using both hands in a smooth, powerful stroke. He resheathed the blade and took the cane out of his belt. Fiel ran up to take it and set it gently against the wall.

"I need a lovely assistant or a brave volunteer," Galhardo said.

I'd been watching him closely, so I never had a chance to notice Sage creeping up behind me. When she shoved me in the back, it caught me totally by surprise. I stumbled forward into the circle.

"Excellent!" Galhardo beamed up into my face. He was almost a foot shorter than me and just over half my weight. I'd seen him fight and he was good, but standing in front of me he looked like a little kid.

"*Chuugi,*" he said, "I want you to punch me in the face."

"Come on, Galhardo, I mean *Yuuki*. I don't want to punch you."

"Don't worry," he said. His smile quirked into a cocky grin, "You won't."

"All right," I said. I swung my fist, aiming for a point just beside his head. I didn't want to hurt him if he made a mistake.

Galhardo didn't move. My fist swept harmlessly past him. The momentum of the punch meeting nothing made me step forward to catch my balance. I steadied myself while the others looked on.

"Don't punch *at* me, noob," he said. "Punch me!"

Something about the way he called me a noob or the cheesy grin that still played across his face made me see red. Maybe it was the frustration from days of being in danger and not knowing what was going on. Whatever the reason, I dug my heels into the ground and put all 270 pounds of me into the punch I threw right at the bridge of his nose. He'd asked for it and I was ready to give it to him.

The next thing I saw was the lights in the dojo's ceiling. I was lying on my back at Galhardo's feet, sputtering and struggling to get my breath back. As my punch came in, Galhardo had moved his hand just like drawing his sword. The movement made his wrist connect with mine and moved my fist just enough to miss his face. Then he'd grabbed my wrist with both hands and swung down like a sword chop. He used my force and slammed me onto the straw mats hard enough to knock the wind out of me.

I lay there, coughing, until the stars cleared out of my eyes. I'm a wrestler. I can take a fall, but *Yuuki* had moved so quickly I was on the ground before I had even realized I was going down. When my head cleared, I heard Sensei. He was speaking to Galhardo in a stern tone.

"*Yuuki,* you threw too hard. You had no control. Hips should be *so*. Elbows *so*."

I felt badly for him. I'd thrown a hard punch and I'd deserved to fall hard. I crawled to my feet and said "Sensei, I'm all right."

"No matter," Sensei said. He turned slightly to include everybody in the lesson. "No matter if he hurt you. If *Yuuki* throws you hard, okay. If he throws you soft, okay. As long as he throws you how he wants to throw you. If he throws by accident, no good."

Sensei adjusted Galhardo's shoulders and hips gently, despite the harshness of his words. He demonstrated something with a sharp whip of his wrists then beckoned me forward.

"Try again."

I punched at *Yuuki* again, as hard as the last time but without the anger. He threw me even harder. As I spun through the air, though, he pulled gently on my arm just before I landed. I hit the mat with much less force. It was still enough to know that I'd just fallen down, but not enough to actually hurt.

I jumped up and *Yuuki* showed the move in slow motion, explaining just what he'd done and how we should do it. We broke up to practice. *Yuuki* worked with Sensei. Fiel paired off with Alex, leaving me to try it with Sage.

"Just like with Coach Russel," I said, "Get shown, then work it out."

"Just like that."

I tried my best, and by the end I could feel the basics starting to become part of my muscle memory. The trick was to block the punch as gently as possible so Sage wouldn't slow her forward momentum. If she was still moving when I went for the throw, I could launch all 220 pounds of her with no real effort. If she stopped, it would be easier to move a stop sign that was still in the sidewalk.

When Sage threw me, it was like she knew when I was going to move *before* I moved. If I threw with less than my whole weight, she just dodged my fist, but every time I committed, she knew when and where to move my body. She stayed quiet while we practiced, but said plenty with her body, though: mostly things like "fall down," "fall down now," and "fall down hard."

Yuuki called us into a circle again and had each of us demonstrate the move. I managed to make Sage stumble, but she slammed me to the mat almost as hard as *Yuuki* had during the first demonstration.

"*Chuugi*," *Yuuki* said. "How did she do that?"

"I don't know. She moved so fast."

"It's not that she moved faster than you. You're fast, and not just fast for somebody your size. She moved *sooner* than you. She moved *first*."

"What, now?

"Most of us know about this, but it's good to review. It's like this. When Sage attacks you, you respond to her moving. When you attack Sage, she responds to your *wanting to move*."

"Are you telling me she used the Force?"

"Kind of," *Yuuki* said. Next to me, Galhardo smiled. I was guessing he either liked *Star Wars* or thought I was an idiot, but it could have been both. "It's like this. Look at me."

I did. I saw a small, dark kid with a game leg that didn't stop him from being more graceful than I was on my best days.

"Not with your eyes. *Look* at me with your heart, with your *dan tian.*"

"My *dan tian*?"

Sensei spoke from his place at the side of the mat. He hadn't moved since *Yuuki* had called us back together. "Your *dan tian* is your center of chi, the energy you share with the universe. It's just below your navel, nearer to the spine. You feel emotions and truths there before you feel them in your heart or your brain."

I thought about that and how my … *dan tian* … felt larger during perfect moments like before a match or during good days with my mom. I closed my eyes, breathed in and focused on that part of me and it responded to my focus, seeming to grow until it filled my body completely. I opened my eyes.

"Whoa," was all I could say. *Yuuki* was surrounded by a nimbus of blue light that covered his body like a close suit. When he saw my face and laughed, the light sparkled with gold flashes.

"There you go," he said. "Keep *looking.*" Then he threw a lightning-fast punch toward my head.

An instant before his hand started to move, his halo of light turned a shade darker and extended a spike toward my face. With that warning, it was easy to sidestep, capture his arm and throw him to the mat with plenty of time to spare.

"Wahoo!" Galhardo shouted.

"I told you he was a fast learner," Sage said.

Yuuki picked himself up off the mat and looked at each of us in turn. "Go forth and do likewise."

Sage and I practiced together for another ten minutes or so. Sometimes the *looking* trick worked for me and other times I couldn't keep the focus with such a big, dangerous person throwing punches at my favorite nose. But I felt I was getting the hang of it and that I could practice it later. I wondered if I could apply the concept to competition on the wrestling team.

Practice ended sooner than I wanted, but about 10 minutes after my shoulder and elbow were ready to quit. We lined up and bowed, again chanting "*Gi, Yuuki, Jin, Rei, Makoto, Meiyo, Chuugi.*" Then we were done.

CHAPTER SEVENTEEN

Sensei called me over when class ended. Everybody else bowed off the deck and talked quietly as they got ready to leave. I noticed they all wore sandals despite the chilly weather. Easier to slip on and off during class, I guessed.

I jogged over to Sensei, "Yes, sir?"

"What do you know about what chased you last night?"

"You all called them *oni*. I guess that's what they are."

"Knowing something's name doesn't mean knowing the thing itself. Often, just the opposite. Can you come with me?"

Sensei led me up a narrow staircase and through a trapdoor to the roof. It was afternoon in the middle of a Portland winter, and light was already beginning to fade from the sky. He led me to the edge of the building. Below us, I could see the park we'd fled through the night before.

"*Chuugi,* what do you see in the park?" he asked.

"Some kids are skateboarding in the basketball court. There's a street person sleeping on a bench, a lady walking her dog. A couple's talking by that tree."

"What else?"

I scanned the park for other things worth noticing, but unless he wanted me to mention each blade of grass or something like that, I really had nothing to mention. "What am I looking for?"

"Do you remember how you *looked* in class a moment ago?"

"Yes," I thought back to the way Sage's desire to knock me on my butt seemed to extend beyond her, to the colors that surrounded her while we sparred.

"*Look* at the park. See what's there, *Chuugi*. Not just what you expect to see."

I closed my eyes and tried to access the power that had let me see the energy around Sage. It was like grabbing at a fish in a stream, but I did catch it. I caught it and pulled it into myself and something changed inside my mind. The same as when you stick your head underwater and everything sounds different. I opened my eyes and jumped backward in shock.

Oni were in the park. A thin one with a long snout rode piggyback on one of the skateboarding kids. Another crouched in the trees above the talking couple, drooping long tentacles down onto their heads. The street person seemed buried in them, with three or four *oni* boiling around him like, well, like a litter of demons feeding on somebody too weak to resist.

I turned to Sensei and almost jumped back again. He was glowing with a white light so bright it almost burned. I blinked and the light was gone. When I turned to look back at the park, the *oni* were gone, too.

"Did I imagine all that?"

"No," he said. "I sometimes suspect that we imagine what you're seeing now. But what you saw for that moment was real. You can do that if you choose to look with your entire self and not let your mind or eyes judge what they tell you. Bushido Champions have that power."

"There were *oni*. In the park. They were on top of people."

"Yes," Sensei walked back to the trap door and down the stairs. I followed.

As we reached the bottom, I thought of the bright light coming from Sensei. If the *oni* were real, that must have been real, too. I said, "Sensei, who are you?"

"I'm your teacher, *Chuugi*. I'll see you next week."

CHAPTER EIGHTEEN

I put on my shoes and stepped through the little front shop, my mind hazy with what I'd seen and learned. It felt like the more I knew, the less I understood. My brain told me it was all impossible, that these "Bushido Champions" had to be some kind of cult like Cael said, that I was going to end up drinking Kool-Aid with flowers in my hair. But I'd seen the *oni* with my own eyes, and something in the center of me told a different story than the one in my head.

Sage was standing on the porch when I got outside. She had one hand on a lion-dog statue, rubbing its head and scratching it between the ears. When I came out, she said "Going home?"

"Yeah. I mean, I guess so. I hadn't thought to do anything else."

"Sensei wanted me to walk with you, to help explain some things."

"I think I'd like that very much." I'd gotten so much information in the last 12 hours or so, but none of it added up to actual knowledge. I needed some context, somebody who knew to slow down when explaining stuff to me.

We started walking together down the sidewalk. The winter wind rattled bare branches above us, and I hunched in on myself under my light sweats. Damp air hissed around us, sounding like the ocean.

"The *oni* ..." I began.

"Calling them *oni* is like saying something is an insect. There are lots of different kinds."

"You mean like how some look like crows and others look like gophers?"

"Exactly, *Kenku* and *Tanuki*, those two. Also, *oni* is what the Japanese call them, but they're everywhere. Other cultures call them demons, or *loa*, or *wendigo*. But they're all the same brand of nasty."

"And *yokai*?"

"You were paying attention," she shot me an approving glance. "There are stronger demons and weaker demons. *Oni* are the littlest, the most common."

"Sensei took me to the roof and showed me how to see them, like I'd been able to see you wanting to smash me. Half the people in the park had an *oni* on them. This homeless guy was totally covered."

Sage winced. As we walked, she drifted closer to me, leaning against me in the wind. Her voice was a whisper. "That's right. Usually less than half of people have one, but a public park on a winter night isn't exactly the happiest place ever. People with better places to be usually aren't in one."

"Why does that matter?"

"*Oni* don't eat or drink. Or maybe I should say they

eat emotions. Negative emotions, like the opposites of what our names stand for. Fear. Jealousy. Hatred. Sadness. Loneliness. Things like that."

"That's why there were so many on the street person?"

"Maybe," she said. She touched my arm. We didn't stop walking, but her body language changed to say what came next would be important. I listened as hard as I knew how. "Or maybe it's the other way around."

"What?"

"It's why *oni* are dangerous. They're tricky. If they can catch hold of you, they'll whisper into your ears. Your body and mind won't hear them, but your soul will. They'll tell you lies and half-truths, make you jealous or afraid or sad. It's possible he's homeless because he has so many *oni* on him."

"And if they did that to the guy in the park, it's more than just our school with the problem?"

"Absolutely. There are *oni* everywhere, all the time. Not usually so many. That probably has to do with the *yokai*, but they're around and they take advantage of any situation."

"How?"

"You ever fly?"

"Once to Disneyland. I was 10."

"Terrorists blew up a building more than 10 years ago. That's awful enough, but how many excited, happy people are at the airport these days?"

"None. There never are."

"Not anymore, at least that's what my dad says. One bad thing happened — the attacks on 9/11 — but *oni* manipulated people's responses so now the whole country is a little bit sadder. There's less joy in the world."

I didn't remember how airports were before 2001, but I'd heard my mom complain about that, too. "Wow."

"And it's a cycle. The *oni* make pain happen, which creates a sadder world, which makes it that much easier for them to make more pain happen. Rinse, repeat."

"Is that what happened to DuPree?"

"Yes."

"How do they get inside?"

"You have to let them in. If they're nearby when you have a really dark moment, they can slip inside your head. Then they control you. Dupree's always been an angry dude. I've known him since grade school. When you took his spot, it was just the kind of opportunity an *oni* would use."

We reached my building and stopped at the bottom of the stairs. I said, "This is me."

"Okay," Sage said. She shuffled from foot to foot in front of me in the winter wind.

"There's more, isn't there?" I asked.

"Lots more."

"Can you come up for a while?"

"Sure. I have to be home by 5 sharp for dinner, but Mom won't worry until then."

I led her up the stairs and let us in. The first thing I saw was my computer screen with a message from Susan.

PdxSusan: Whatever, loser. Were there really cops?

I crossed our little living room and typed a response.

Me: Really. Can we have lunch tomorrow?

PdxSusan is offline.

Sage had come with me and was looking over my shoulder. "Susan Parker, huh?" She shoulder-checked me hard enough to push me away from the table.

"Yeah, I guess."

"Fast. She used to kick my ass in sprints during soccer."

"I bet. She looks it."

"So, what's the story there?"

"I wish I knew."

"Fibber," she poked me in the chest with one strong finger.

"Seriously. I have no idea, ask her. Jut promise to tell me what you find out."

"Ah. You're in that space." She glanced around the room. "Where are your parents?"

I told her about my dad and his meth habit, and Mom going to Eugene to testify. I don't tell people about that stuff, but Sage felt safe. It's like that sometimes when you practice with somebody. You share something important to both of you that other people don't know. It happens fast, and I trusted Sage about as much as I trusted anybody besides Mom.

Sage said, "Oh. So that's why she, on the phone … with the drugs."

"Yep."

"I'm so sorry. That must be … um. I'm sorry, *Chuugi.*"

We stood for a moment, there in front of the computer. She was very close to me. Susan hadn't logged back in yet or at least wasn't bothering to respond to my message.

A question came back to me that I'd thought of on the way to practice. I probably should have asked it earlier, but the past few hours had been busy. "Sage, do you like me?"

She gave me a look, and I suddenly realized the two of us were alone together in my apartment. The space suddenly felt very small. I coughed and cleared my throat. "I don't mean *like* me like me. I mean, would you be sad if I died? If I, say, were eaten by horrible shadow demons?"

She didn't laugh, but she didn't hit me, either. "Why yes, Connor. That would make me sad."

"Then why did you wait until last night to clue me in? I would have been safer if I'd known the first time you guys rescued me."

"It's not that simple," she said. "People who know about *oni* are more vulnerable to them. I don't know why, exactly. If you're ignorant, all they can do is mess with your head. If you know, they can attack you physically. If we'd told you before we were certain you were one of us, it would put you in real danger."

"Ooookay."

"Like I said, it's confusing. And there's more. A *yokai* will attack whoever it wants. If it knew who you were because it was watching us, it might have gone after your family while we were saving you."

It didn't make less sense than a dozen other things I'd started believing that weekend. I went to sit on the couch. Sage hesitated for a moment then settled on a chair.

I said, "How do we beat them?"

"If they're just talking, you can't do much. They're like smoke. If you tell them to leave, they have to go. It's trickier than I'm making make it sound. If they're inside somebody, you have to make them come out. You can stun or knock out the person they're riding, or you can tempt them out."

"I thought they tempted us?"

"Yes, but negative emotions control them just as much as they feed them. It's like being addicted to a drug, I guess. If you make one angry or afraid, or if you inflict enough pain, it will jump right out of a person. When it does that, it's in solid form for a few seconds. We can get it good when it's solid."

"Like at the baseball diamond, when Galhardo cut the badger … the, uh, *Tanuki*."

"Yes. Sometimes they'll turn solid on their own in order to attack, but that's been rare so far."

I wanted to ask more questions, but there was too much information to get a hold on any one thing. My brain kept slipping on concepts until I felt more confused than when I'd started. So much for Sage making things easier. After a while I just said, "Whoa."

"That's exactly what I said when I found out."

"How long ago was that?"

"Last summer. Fiel and Galhardo were already with Sensei. Alex joined up just before Halloween." She looked at her watch. "4:00 on the dot. I'll head out. See you in practice, huh?" She was up and out the door before I could get off the couch.

I went to my room and changed out of my workout

clothes. They were wet with sweat and Portland winter. Kyle stared at me from his poster as if to say, "Nothing's impossible. Just look at me."

"Good point," I said aloud.

I made dinner out of leftovers then watched a sitcom on Netflix. Between episodes, I put my window screen right and double-locked the front door. Outside, shadows moved and flickered along the walls and street. They looked normal, though, moving the way I expected shadows to move on a windy night. At least that's what I kept telling myself.

With Mom in Eugene and my dad in jail, I felt very much alone. For all that connection I'd felt earlier, the Bushido Champions were all far away. If something came for me, I would have no back-up. Nobody to save me if things went wrong.

Around 8:00, Susan's message box popped up with "Okay." She logged out before I could respond.

CHAPTER NINETEEN

Ponderosa looked like a high school should: all red brick with wide stairs and tall windows. Most high schools in Portland look like that. It's one of the things I like about the city. In a lot of places the newer high schools are built with flat slabs of concrete that look more like prisons. I should know. I've seen plenty of both.

Pausing in front of the school, I closed my eyes, breathed and found my *dan tian*. It was getting easier each time I tried. *Oni* covered the whole building. They flocked like pigeons by the doors, swooping down on students as they came in from buses and cars. It made me want to cry. So many of my classmates, even the ones I didn't know or like, were weighted down by the whispering shadows. I got off my bike and walked it to the bike rack, watching as flocks of misery used my school for a hunting ground.

As I locked up my bike I saw the same Subaru wagon I'd ridden home in Saturday night. Alex was in the passenger seat next to an older woman with the same pale skin and hair. I called to Alex as she got out and she waited for me to catch up. I was still *looking,* and I could see a little core of light inside her, like Sensei's but not as bright. She smiled when she saw me, but her face fell as I got closer.

"Turn it off," she said.

"What?"

"You couldn't resist, could you?" She wasn't exactly shouting, but her voice sounded angry and sad. "You're *looking*. That's why your face is like you're in the middle of a nightmare and you can't wake up.

I stared at her. Was that what I looked like? I mean, sure, seeing all the *oni* hit me where it hurt, but I could handle that. I'd handled tougher things. Wrestling, moving, my dad, but Alex knew stuff I didn't.

"It's that obvious?"

"Yes. Turn it off. Turn it off or it will break your heart. It's worse inside."

I scanned the roofline of our school. You could hardly see the edge for all the *oni* scrambling around on it. "How could it possibly be worse?"

"Think about it, *Chuugi*. High school is mostly about being awkward, frustrated, obedient and afraid. We're all worried about our grades and who likes us and what the other kids think. Half the people, and that includes the teachers, don't want to be here at all. And that half does all they can to make things miserable for the other half."

That was a fair enough description of high school from what I'd seen. But that was just life. I didn't see what it had to do with *oni* or with us. "So?"

"*Oni* feed on negative emotions. High school is like an all-you-can-eat buffet for them."

I realized the truth of what she said. A thrill of fear ran up my legs into my stomach. "Wow."

"So turn it off. If you don't, it will make you so sad they'll have a chance to get inside you."

"All right." I wasn't sure how to stop *looking,* I had only done it by accident before, but when I let my focus shift from my center to what Alex thought, I felt that connection disappear. When I opened my eyes, the demons were gone. They'd disappeared from my sight, but not from my memory. Knowing they were there, just beyond my vision, made me shiver.

"Smile, *Chuugi,*" Alex said. She stopped to open the school door for me. "Unless they manifest — "

"Manifest?"

"Become physical. Like they do if you push them out of someone or if they want to kick your butt. Unless they do that, positive feelings are all we have to fight them with." She gave me a sad, pale, brave smile. "At the very least, it has to really tick them off. That's reason enough all by itself."

She glided into the crowds flowing through the hall, her long hair sweeping back and forth with the roll of her graceful walk, moving through them like the other people weren't there at all. Every footstep found just the right place to move her forward without interrupting anybody else's path.

CHAPTER TWENTY

I walked through the Commons, a wide area of concrete benches and milling classmates. In the middle, a dozen or so kids were protesting the war. Most of them wore T-shirts with slogans about peace and death or carried big cards saying the same things. Mr. Orwal, the head of school security, watched them from a spot against the wall by a fire extinguisher. He didn't look nearly as nervous as the riot cops you see on YouTube videos. Mostly, he looked bored.

Despite Alex's warning, I *looked*. The protesters all glowed with a quiet, warm light. Some glowed brighter than others, like Jack Cleaver whose dad had died in the war last year, but they all had it at least a little bit. The light was sad, yet powerful at the same time. That was something to remember: sometimes things hurt, but we can own how we react to the pain.

In class, maybe half of the students had an *oni* at any given time, but it changed throughout the day. Matt Travers had an *oni* during English, but it was gone when I saw him again in math. Neither Steve Leise nor Jennifer Cho had *oni* at the beginning of PE, but both had some when we left for the locker rooms. Of my morning teachers, Mr. Carroll in English and Mrs. Roghan in History had *oni*. Coach Russel, who also taught my PE class, didn't.

Neither did Principal Graff, I saw, when she poked her head into History class to ask for some paperwork. That seemed strange. Of all the adults in the school, she seemed like the perfect candidate for demonic possession. Maybe she liked her strange, quiet, depressing school just the way it was. That might protect her from demons, but if that were true she wasn't all that different from the monsters infesting Ponderosa High.

In history class, I couldn't help but peek at Susan. She wore a plain, loose T-shirt, had her hair in a braid that ran down the middle of her back and carried no *oni*. In fact, she had a little glow like Alex, the glow I'd come to think of as happiness and hope. I wondered if it had anything to do with me.

The halls were dark, strange and terrifying. *Oni* roosted on the tops of lockers or rode on my schoolmates. They leapt from one student to the next to the next, and nobody seemed to notice them at all. In a corner, a small kid with glasses getting ripped on by some jocks was hard to see under the flock of *oni* surrounding him. In another spot, a couple snuck a kiss between classes and their happiness made a point of light that drove nearby *oni* scrambling for darker territory.

I stopped *looking* a little before lunch. Alex had been right. It was all so depressing, and I couldn't do anything about it. It was better to save my energy for fights I could win. I dug my sack lunch out of my backpack and took it to the cafeteria. I always packed my own lunch because school food is so horrible, and I don't mean "horrible" like I'm trying to be funny. I mean it has all the nutrition of fast food with none of the taste. I'm an athlete. You don't give a sports car cheap gas.

Susan was at her usual spot near the center of the room. She saw me and waved me over. When I got close, all her friends but Tasha got up and left. They whispered and giggled to each other as they walked out of sight. My heart beat a little faster and my knees started to sweat, but I sat down.

"Hey there, stud," Tasha said. She was sitting to my right, and she bumped my hip by sliding her rear end along the bench. She wasn't all in black today; instead she was wearing a white T-shirt and jeans with a leather jacket. She looked like Fonzi from *Happy Days*, if Fonzi had facial piercings.

"Uh, hi, Tasha."

"Susan tells me there were police at your place. It's the only reason she's talking to you. Tell me, beefcake, did they have handcuffs?" She winked at me then got up to go.

"Susan," I started.

"Shut up, dork," she said. She didn't even look at me.

My stomach clenched and I felt dark thoughts crowd around me. I wondered if an *oni* had come to perch nearby. I shut up. I'm good at shutting up, even when I don't always know when I should. Besides, my mouth was so dry I couldn't have talked if I wanted to.

CHAPTER TWENTY

Susan finished her cafeteria chicken nuggets then washed them down with a carton of chocolate milk. My stomach got even queasier watching that, but at the same time I liked the way her lips moved as she drank. The way she closed her eyes while she finished the milk made my throat hurt.

She put the carton down and said, "Mr. Morgan. You know, if you don't want to go out with me, there are easier ways to do it."

"That's not it," I stammered. "There really were police. And some guys really did chase me, um … again."

"So you're saying you do want to go out with me?"

"Um, yes? Yes. Most definitely. I want to go out with you. Yes, I would like to do that."

"Okay," she giggled a little and smiled brightly. "I'd like that, too."

"Okay," I chuckled in a distinctly masculine way. I did not giggle like a little girl, not even a little.

"Thursday night, after your match. Let's go to Shari's and you can buy me a milkshake."

"Sounds good."

"Does it, now?" She was laughing at me, just a little, but that was okay.

"Meet me in the hall?"

"Yes. Just dress for the occasion. Or, you know, at least dress."

The bell rang. Susan touched my hand, a short caress that stood all the hairs there on end. Then she hustled off to class. On my way out of the cafeteria, I passed Principal Graff marching at the head of a line of all the protesters from that morning. I *looked* to see flocks of *oni* diving at them, all but swallowing the peaceful glow they'd carried earlier. No *oni* rode on Principal Graff, but she wasn't glowing happily either. Maybe she didn't love busting kids as much as I'd thought.

Mr. Keranovak was at the rear of the line, herding the protesters to whatever Principal Graff had in store for them. He had no *oni* on him, either. He caught me watching and gave me a wink. "Viva la revolución."

After lunch was a lot of the same. I didn't *look* at Mrs. Kellar in psychology or at Mr. Lum in math. They both seemed happy to be there, which might be one reason I always liked their classes best. In the hall, between math and wrestling practice, Susan passed me a note with a heart drawn on it. I tucked it into my breast pocket, over my heart.

CHAPTER TWENTY-ONE

Here's how it is on a wrestling team. On game day, coaches try to get everybody a match, but only one athlete in each weight class gets to count toward the team score. Those wrestlers go last, on a single mat at the center of the room, under spotlights, with the whole crowd watching. That's the varsity team.

At the beginning of the season, coaches pick who's on varsity. Different coaches use different methods, but they all choose who they think is the best wrestler in each weight class. They do that a week or two before the first match of the season, usually sometime between Halloween and Thanksgiving.

But here's the thing: anybody who wants to can challenge the varsity guy. If you win the match, you're on varsity until somebody challenges and beats you. It's how I got DuPree's slot after moving to Ponderosa in the middle of the season. Otherwise, there's no way a new guy could walk onto the competition team in just a couple of weeks. Coach Russel allowed challenges every Monday. When I got to the wrestling room, I saw DuPree was going to try exactly that. A whiteboard high on the far wall read:

WRESTLE-OFFS
Ortiz vs. Roman
N'golo vs. Smith
DuPree vs. Morgan

DuPree stopped wrestling with his partner long enough for me to notice him giving me the stink eye. I mouthed "bring it." He got back to warming up. Sage grabbed me and we started rolling, going for low shots and deep sprawls. We moved slowly to get our muscles ready for the action in practice.

"What's the story with DuPree?" I asked. "He wants to take me on for the varsity spot, but he doesn't seem mad about Thursday. You know, that time you beat him into unconsciousness before he and his pals could kick me to death."

"He probably doesn't remember," Sage said. *Remember* came out in a groan as I slammed her to the mat.

"How? If I tried to kill a guy and an Amazon princess stopped me, it seems like something I'd remember."

"It's not that simple," Sage grunted. We were in a clinch, each of us cranking on the other's neck with one hand, trying to establish a meaningful hold with the other. "He can't explain what happened, even though he probably has foggy memories of the whole thing. He doesn't know about the *oni*. His brain will tell him he got drunk or had a bad dream. After an *oni* rides somebody, most people fall asleep. Like you're doing right now!"

She ducked between my legs and threw me on my face with a fireman's throw. I landed hard then rolled free to go again.

"Nice one, Kaiser!" Coach Russel called from halfway across the room. It was amazing how often he caught moments like that.

Sage gave him a thumbs-up and closed with me to go again.

If you're wrestling a challenge match, Coach lets you skip conditioning at the end of practice. I got some water in the hall and *looked* around the cool, mostly empty hallway. DuPree was at one end, staring at a wall and muttering to himself. I could see an *oni* hanging on his back, digging its claws into him like a koala bear climbing a tree. An evil koala bear that eats souls instead of whatever it is koala bears eat. Far away at the other end of the hall, Mr. Keranovak mopped the floor. He was whistling to himself, and still *oni*-free. Interesting that a war veteran who grew up in some kind of nightmare country would have no *oni*, but a teenager from America was an easy mark. It went to show something, though I couldn't say exactly what.

The first two matches went about how I expected. Though I'd only been on the team for a few weeks, I'd gotten to know everybody's strengths and weaknesses. Ortiz was a new guy like me, in from a championship team in the Cascade Mountains. He beat Roman with a pin in the first round. N'golo lost his challenge, leaving

Smith at varsity for the 145 weight class. Coach held up Smith's hand and both wrestlers walked off the mat. Then it was my turn.

DuPree shook my hand at the center of the mat. He looked determined, psyched up, but nothing else. He had no sign of the homicidal hatred he'd shown Thursday night. Maybe Sage was right about him not remembering. Coach blew the whistle. We circled each other. Lightweights — like Ortiz and Roman — are all energy and movement. They run across the mat, tumble and roll with each other. Heavyweights move more slowly and when we take somebody down it's usually with a single, decisive move. Our physiologies are different, so we fight a different game.

I shot for DuPree's legs. He sprawled away and landed on my shoulders with all 280 of his pounds. It slammed me face-first into the mat and his legs sprang out of my grip. He pivoted on top of me to get behind and score a takedown. Score 2 DuPree, zip for Morgan. I tried to fight my way out, but he held me for the rest of the round.

Zero-two at the break, and DuPree won the toss. He took top position and slammed into me when Coach blew his whistle. I took most of the fall on my face, and stars shot through my vision. DuPree snaked his arm under mine to grab my head and turn me over, but I wiped it off. I muscled up to my hands and knees, and he hit me again. I fell hard and saw stars. Again. I wiped his hands clear, struggled with his whole weight on me and got back on all fours.

I remembered the lesson at the dojo and focused on my *dan tian*. Just like at the beginning of a match, it felt heavier, easier to reach. A moment after I made the connection, I felt DuPree's intent to slam me again moving ahead of his body. I angled my back just enough to turn his slam into a glancing blow. He slid across my back and I sprang into a forward roll. We came out with me on top and DuPree on his back. Two points reversal. Dupree struggled and rolled, keeping at least one shoulder off the mat for the rest of the round. He didn't get loose, but he didn't let me pin. I got three points for the near fall, and the round ended at 5 for me, 2 for him. I chose neutral position, both of us standing, to start the final round.

DuPree's breath was ragged, his face flushed. He was running out of gas. I wasn't. One thing about biking to and from school: no matter how hard everybody else was working, nobody cycled four miles every day on top of that. Nobody but me.

I danced in and out, moving like a 150-pounder. It wasn't something I could do for long, but I was betting I could do it for longer than DuPree. He tried to keep up, but his feet moved more and more heavily with every step. Soon they started to drag. I shot low, grabbed his ankle and stood up with it still in my hands. I didn't even have to sweep his other leg. DuPree fell and I got on top. Two more points. Coach blew the whistle and I won, 7-2.

We shook hands. DuPree wasn't happy, but he knew it was fair. "See you next week," was all he said.

"I'll be here."

Coach raised my hand above my head to signal my victory. It wasn't a real match, but that's what you do. It's a wrestling thing.

CHAPTER TWENTY-TWO

I pushed myself hard all the way back to our apartment, even on the uphill stretch past the community center. The cold air burned in my lungs. It made me cough, but I kept the pace. Like I said, it's the reason I'm in better shape than DuPree. My record was just over five minutes for the two miles. As I pulled into the parking lot, I saw Mom's car. I shut my bike up in our storage space and closed the padlock on the door. It took me a few minutes because padlocks always give me trouble. Mom would say that it's my big galoot fingers and compare them to her small, deft nurse's hands.

The lights were off when I came through the door. Mom was sitting at our kitchen table, smoking a cigarette. She didn't usually smoke anymore, had quit when she was pregnant with me. But sometimes she said it was smoke or go crazy — usually after she'd seen my father.

"Mom?" I said.

She didn't answer. She was staring out the window looking at something that wasn't in the room. Her eyes were red and her face was puffy from crying.

I stepped closer, moving slowly so I wouldn't startle her. "Mom?"

She turned and saw me. "Hey, kiddo." Her voice was almost as small and pale as Alex's.

"How'd it go?"

"The sentence is seven years. He might be out in three." She stood to grind out her cigarette in the bottom of our sink, then ran water to flush the ashes.

"Three years?"

"Yeah. Long enough maybe for him to make the right changes. Long enough for we two to get ourselves together." She looked so small and beaten. I knew it was hard for her to see my dad, that she still loved who he had been before the drugs, that she felt like every time she testified against him she was betraying the husband who my father had stopped being years ago.

"You could graduate without us moving again. I could get ahead on the bills. It's awful that this had to happen, but ... but ..." her voice trailed off.

I said, "But there's good coming out of it."

"Whatever you say, kiddo." She tried to smile, but mostly failed at it.

I had a terrible thought. I focused my attention and *looked*. Two *oni* crouched on my mother's shoulders. They looked like angry black cats whispering hate into her ears. Standing beside my Mom, I felt how we shared our energies, how our chi were mixed together. I saw the feelings, a part of my mom's soul, seeping out of her and into their greedy little mouths.

Almost running to where she stood, I took both of Mom's hands in mine. Alex had said positive emotions are our weapon against the *oni*. I pulled her to me and hugged her hard, squeezing like she sometimes told me I'd squeeze her when I was a baby and she was my whole, wide world.

Right next to my face, the *oni* squirmed like they were in pain. They kept whispering. I couldn't hear the words, but I knew what thoughts they were twisting through my mother's heart and head.

"I'm glad you're home, Mom," I said. "I love you."

One of the demons gave a scream I could hear only in my mind, like Pizza Guy had during the chase on Saturday night. I hugged Mom closer, bending far over to bury my head right where one of the *oni* stood on her shoulder. I said into her ear, "Don't let him get under your skin like that, Mom. He made his decisions, and he'll keep paying for them as long as he acts the way he does. It's not your fault."

Mom's arms tightened around me, squeezing me by the waist. The *oni* squirmed on their perches, but they still held tight to their prey. My mother. I felt my own energy darken and curdle as it flowed together with my mother's emotions and thoughts.

"I know you did the right thing, Mom. I know it was hard."

Mom didn't respond. She just stood there in my arms, feeling awful and feeding the *oni*. Anger at the demons, and at my dad, coursed hot through me and I wanted to reach out and smash the little monsters. I breathed deeply, focused on my *dan tian* and imagined the bright energy there washing out the dark.

I said to my mother, the person I loved most in the world, "I'm proud of you."

A silver light started to shine from inside my mother, a tiny glimmer just above her hips. It felt warm in the same way Sage's and DuPree's intent had felt hot. It grew brighter as I held her, chasing away the darker currents. The *oni* leapt away as if she'd suddenly become scalding hot. They clung to the wall behind her. I pinned them with my hardest glare and growled "Never" into the dim room.

Something about my anger, and my worry for Mom, gave that word the same power I'd heard in Sage and Fiel that first night. Both *oni* skittered along the ceiling and out through the window Mom had cracked open for her smoke.

"Never what, honey?" Mom asked. She squeezed me one more time, then leaned back to look at my face.

"Nothing, Ma. I just never like seeing you in this state. Your ex-husband's not worth it."

Mom smiled. It was a sad smile, but still a smile. The little light at her center didn't fade. She wiped her eyes and leaned over to turn on the kitchen light. "Well, he gave me you. That's worth something. What's for dinner?"

"I didn't spend all the money you left for me. There should be enough for Thai food from around the corner."

Mom's light grew even brighter. "That's my boy."

CHAPTER TWENTY-THREE

Bploink.

Mom was in bed, and I was heading that way soon. I could still taste pad thai and yellow curry in the back of my mouth. Susan was on the chat with me. All things considered, it was turning out to be a pretty okay night.

PdxSusan: You're not going to ditch on me again Thursday, are you?

Me: No. Definitely not. Uh-uh.

Not if I could help it. For all I knew, Thursday afternoon would put me in between the boogeyman and the chupacabra while Thor and Chuck Norris fought over who got to break my wishbone once I was dead. At the rate things were going, that was maybe even likely. But they'd have to wait until after my date with Susan. They could take a number.

PdxSusan: Good. You're on thin ice, buddy, and I don't want to have to train up a replacement crush just yet.

PdxSusan: :-)

Me: So you _do_ have a crush on me?

PdxSusan: Maybe.
Me: I'll be there. Count on it.
PdxSusan: Really?
Me: Really.
PdxSusan: Promise?
Me: Unless the world ends, and maybe even then.
PdxSusan: OK. I like that.
Me: See you tomorrow?
PdxSusan: Unless the world ends.
PdxSusan: And maybe even then.
PdxSusan is offline.

CHAPTER TWENTY-FOUR

Sage grabbed me by the collar first thing Tuesday morning before I'd even started looking for Susan. She slammed me into the nearest locker, sending a pack of freshman girls scattering in all directions, and put her face very close to mine.

"Did you hear? Coach Russel got suspended! Principal Graff kicked him out of the school!"

"What?" I felt like she'd just punched me in the gut. "Why?"

"I don't know. I just heard because my mom works in the district office. He's down there right now filing a complaint."

"What about practice?"

"Coach Vigil will be there, but screw that. What about Coach?"

"Ahem," said a voice behind Sage. I peered over her shoulder to see Susan's face. Both her eyebrows were arched — not in a way that said she thought something was funny. Sage let me go, but Susan was down the hall before I even started to move.

"Sorry, *Chuugi,*" Sage said.

"She's already jealous of you, you know," I said. I walked with Sage, figuring I'd never catch Susan if she didn't want to be caught.

"Really?" Sage asked. I couldn't be sure, but I thought she was smiling.

"Yeah. I mean, really. You and I have had way more close bodily contact than me and Susan. We're even wearing less clothing when we do it."

"I'm sorry to hear that."

"Hey, now. Plus there's the wrestling buddies thing. Seriously, she keeps calling you my girlfriend."

Every visible piece of Sage's skin was bright red. Before I could stop her, she darted into the nearest bathroom. A second later, she ran out and scooted into the girls' bathroom next door. I shrugged and headed for class. Understanding Susan was hard enough.

"Sports this week include away games for boys' basketball, girls' volleyball and swim …"

At the start of first period, Carter Robinson droned over the loudspeaker as he read through the morning announcements. When I'd first come to Ponderosa, Carter's show had more of a "morning zoo" radio feel, but over the weeks it had become flat and dry.

"Home matches for girls' basketball on Wednesday and wrestling on Thursday. Come support your schoolmates …"

It was another piece of joy that had disappeared from our school. I wondered if the *yokai* was responsible and, if so, in whom the *yokai* was hiding.

"Tickets are just two dollars …"

That was one part of being in this secret war: it was hard to know what bad stuff happened because of demons and what happened because sometimes life is hard and people can be mean. A new voice interrupted my thoughts: Principal Graff's.

"Ladies and gentlemen," her voice was strong and grating over the loudspeaker. "The custodial staff has brought my attention to a disturbing fact. It seems that our cafeteria tables and floor have an alarming amount of litter on them after each lunch period. This might pass in other schools, but it is not acceptable at Ponderosa High. For the remainder of the week, as a consequence, there is to be no talking during lunch periods. If, by Friday's spirit assembly, you have all learned to take pride in your eating space, the speaking ban will be lifted."

There was a click and the speaker went silent. So did everybody in the room. I'd never heard of that happening in any school, anywhere. Not in schools I'd been to, not in schools I'd visited. Judging by the reactions around me neither had anybody else. Even Mr. Carroll just stared at the speaker with his mouth slightly open.

A moment later, Principal Graff's voice started up again.

"Ladies and gentlemen, I have a sad announcement to make. Mr. Russel, one of our physical education teachers and our head wrestling coach, is taking a leave of absence effective immediately. I know many of you will have questions about this, but you must remember that idle speculation and spreading rumors can only hurt his reputation and memory. Please be respectful and refrain from such behavior until, when and if, Mr. Russel can return to us and answer your questions in his own, uniquely direct fashion."

My stomach felt tight and raw. In the back, Jordan Walker turned his eyes to the ceiling and let out a long sigh. Nobody said a word, which was probably good. It looked like we were all going to need the practice.

I spent most of English class staring at Susan and feeling the knot grow in my stomach. She was sitting next to me, staring straight ahead. I wrote her a note while Mr. Carroll wasn't looking.

That announcement about Coach. That's what Sage was talking to me about.

Susan didn't even look at me when I finally worked up the guts to slip the note onto her desk. She ignored it for most of class, but eventually opened it and wrote something on the bottom. When the bell rang, she threw the paper onto my desk on her way out. I read it as I walked toward the gym for PE.

☹ *I'm not talking to you until tomorrow.*

CHAPTER TWENTY-FIVE

I sat next to Fiel in the cafeteria and ate my peanut butter and banana sandwich in the new, eerie quiet. Fiel had some kind of colorful salad. So did his brother, who sat across the table from us. We ate in silence, looking down at the table like a group of inmates. Principal Graff's rule was in full effect.

Fiel nudged me with an elbow. He jerked his head toward a group of tables at one end of the long room. I glanced at him and shrugged, the body language equivalent of a question mark. He pointed, indicating a clear spot on the cafeteria bench where somebody sitting could look at the flag as he ate. I didn't see anything special.

"Okay," I whispered, "I give. What am I seeing?"

"It's what you're *not* seeing. That's Jack Cleaver's spot."

He was right. Jack sat there most days, eating a school lunch and looking at the flag. I glanced around the room, but didn't see him anywhere else.

Mr. Orwal walked past and behind us. We focused on our lunches, chewing and swallowing with intense concentration until he passed us by. I looked across the cafeteria at Susan, sitting in a quiet knot of her friends. She had her hair up now, and I could see the lines of her cheek and jaw. She looked smart and tough. I hoped she was enough of both to understand about Sage and me earlier that morning.

As soon as Mr. Orwal was out of earshot, Galhardo whispered with his lips apart, his teeth not moving. "Jack lost it this morning. Completely blew a gasket. Started going off about civil rights, and freedom of speech, and how his dad hadn't died for this kind of thing to happen."

"Oh, no," I mouthed.

"Oh, yes. He's gone. After the protest yesterday, he's probably expelled."

"It keeps getting better and better," I whispered, "but how much worse can it get?"

"Remember Columbine?" Fiel said.

I flinched. We'd all been babies when it happened and there had been worse school shootings since, but the massacre at Columbine, Colorado, was one of the first and worst. It was a boogeyman we all knew well, like Pearl Harbor and 9/11.

Like Sage had said, things like that are awful but what comes next is worse. News, political speeches and new laws spread from that kind of thing. It covered the country, even the world, in sadness and despair. Since *oni* feed off emotions like that, something happening at Ponderosa could make the demons more powerful everywhere in the world.

"We can't let that happen," I said.

"I'll get right on that," Galhardo said, "as soon as we figure out where, and who, the *yokai* is."

Mr. Orwal came to stand directly behind us. He still looked bored, but that didn't make him any less intimidating. I'd finished my sandwich, so I sat and fiddled with my lunch sack as he stared down at the three of us. Galhardo and Fiel got quiet, too, their heads down and their jaws crunching on salad.

I thought about silence and how it can get to you after a while. I remembered how quiet the house would get after my dad hit Mom enough times that she stopped crying. Even if I turned up the TV all the way, the house still felt silent. Some kinds of quiet you can't wash away just with noise.

Something bumped my arm. I jumped a little then saw Fiel nudging me. Mr. Orwal had moved on again.

"Um, bro ..." Fiel said, "you've got a little something on your shoulder."

I turned my head and looked, saw nothing, then *looked*. An *oni,* one that looked like a snail the size of a small puppy, was perching there getting fat on my dark memories. Its little antennae waved in the breeze and pulsated. I tried to slap it away, but my hand passed right through like it wasn't even there.

"It hasn't manifested," Galhardo whispered. He'd seen *oni* before — fought them even, fought them with me — but his eyes were wide and white as he *looked* at the *oni* feasting on me.

Fiel rapped the table softly with the knuckles of one hand. "Connor, my man, what's a snail say when he's riding on the back of a turtle?" He was whispering, but somehow managed to say it with a cheesy Vaudeville comedian voice like Fozzie Bear from *The Muppet Show*.

"Oh jeez, Fiel. Not now," I groaned.

"No, really. Is there a better time? I ask you again, *meu amigo*, what's a snail say when he's riding on the back of a turtle?"

"Are you calling him a turtle?" Galhardo asked.

"Hush, you."

I stared at the demon as it sat on my shoulder, sucking on my brain waves. I sighed. "Okay, okay. I don't know, Fiel. What does a snail say when he's riding on the back of a turtle?"

"Wheeeeee!" said Fiel, loudly enough to make Mr. Orwal's head snap around to glare at us from the far end of the table.

It was a total groaner, and it made me groan. Mr. Orwal stared at us. Even though the joke was bad, and Mr. Orwal scared me a little, it made me laugh and the *oni* started hopping from one foot to the other as if I'd grown too hot to stand on.

Across the way Susan looked up. Maybe she'd heard Fiel, too. She saw me see her and, despite herself, smiled just a little before she remembered to stay angry with me. The *oni* sprang off my shoulder and roosted in the ceiling rafters.

"I saw that," Fiel whispered. He elbowed me in the ribs.

"Saw what?"

"Connor and Susan, sitting in a tree," he sang softly.

"Oh, grow up." I said. I punched him in the arm to let him know we were still friends. Across from us, Galhardo laughed quietly into his hands.

CHAPTER TWENTY-SIX

Sage slammed me into the mat hard enough to knock the wind out of me. That was okay. I was getting used to it. When I could breathe again, I crawled to my feet and locked up for another go.

"Jeez, Sage," I grunted. Talking made my stomach hurt. "Don't take it out on me."

"I'm sorry, Morgan. It just makes me so mad. I called Mom at lunch. Coach was suspended because he doesn't like that new silence rule."

"Really?"

"Really. He told Graff what he though, and she booted him."

"She can do that?"

"Apparently." She tried for a hip toss, but I stepped around her feet and skipped away.

"When will he be back?"

"To be determined. Mom says Coach has been around a lot longer than Graff. She can't keep him out, but it will take a hearing or committee or something. He'll be gone at least a couple of weeks."

"Wow. I had no idea a principal had that kind of power. Over adults, I mean."

"Yeah. If Coach wasn't so senior and respected, he wouldn't even get to fight it."

"I'm starting to really dislike that woman."

"Starting?"

"I'm a slow learner." As I said it, Sage ducked beneath my guard and flipped me with the same fireman's carry she'd taken me down with the week before.

"I'll say." She stood still, glaring into space as I got to my feet.

"You don't think …?" I started.

"Don't think what?"

I shook my head. "Nothing. I'm just being stupid."

We clinched up. Sage slapped the back of my head. "Don't do that. Even stupid people can have good ideas, and you're not as dumb as you pretend to be."

"Well, okay. A *yokai* isn't going to possess a student, right? Not one of us. We don't have enough power or access to let it cause the kind of trouble it wants to cause. But I can think of somebody with lots of power. And she can go wherever she wants without anybody stopping her or even wondering why she's there."

Sage let me go, seeming stunned by the idea. I took advantage and dove for her ankles. She sprang away much faster than she should have been able to, landed on my back and pivoted to get the takedown.

"Sucker," she said. "But you have a point. I think we'll need to watch Principal Graff very closely."

"You're only saying that because you want it to be true."

"Maybe, but that doesn't mean it isn't."

CHAPTER TWENTY-SEVEN

I didn't even make it to class Wednesday morning. When I walked in the door, Mr. Orwal intercepted me and escorted me to the front office. Sage was already there, waiting in the line of student chairs along the wall by Principal Graff's office door.

Here's the thing about the principal's office. No matter what school you're in, there's always a pattern to look for when you get called in. It tells you whether you're busted and need to start working on your story or if you're getting some kind of recognition or reward. If the other kids in the office are the smart kids or the good athletes, that means it's a meeting for something good. If they're hoods or thug jocks, you've been called about some scrape or another.

I wasn't sure what Sage and I had done that would get us both into trouble, but it worried me for three reasons. If it had to do with the team, we might lose our wrestling privileges. If it was about the Bushido Champions and Principal Graff was the *yokai*, things could be much worse. Even more scary was how this was yet more time I would be spending with Sage. Susan would not be pleased.

I sat next to her without saying hello. Principal Graff strictly forbade speaking between students in what Galhardo called the "Chairs of Shame." Still, Sage was my friend and I could feel that bond the second I sat down. It was like having a bigger, older, meaner sister on my side. I started to relax.

Principal Graff made us wait through all of first period and most of second before calling us into her office. When we came in, she busied herself at her desk. She made a show of putting everything in order while we waited, letting us know that we were not important. The light in her office was dim, the shadows thick behind her desk. Once she finished, she looked up and spoke to us.

"Mr. Morgan. Miss Kaiser. I've called you in today because I've been given to understand you have some … questions … about your coach's situation."

I opened my mouth, but Principal Graff shot me a look so scary I shut it immediately.

Sage either didn't see it or was immune to the stare. Her voice didn't shake at all as she said, "I'm reasonably certain I understand the situation just fine. Thank you all the same."

Principal Graff sat back like Sage had slapped her. Her face clouded. The room seemed to grow darker and colder. Her voice was sharp. "Then you understand the value of not speaking out of turn about this matter. It can give people the wrong idea and even hurt your coach's good name."

"I understand how that's of value to you. I see nothing in it for me or for Coach or for Morgan here."

"Then your understanding is limited, which is all I can expect of an impertinent teenager. I am afraid I must insist that you refrain from discussing your coach's situation with anybody while you are on school grounds, or with anybody from the school when you're off them."

"My mother works with the district. Are you telling me what I can and can't discuss with my own mom?"

"Let me clarify, Miss Kaiser. The topic is not open for discussion. The consequence of attempting to reopen it could mean your suspension from wrestling or from the school entire. I understand both of you are hoping for scholarships to college when you graduate. That sort of adverse action on your records could seriously undermine your chances."

Principal Graff looked across her wide desk, saying nothing and silently daring us to break the quiet. Sage vibrated with anger next to me, but managed to keep her cool. The clock ticked. Shadows moved on the walls.

I *looked,* expecting to find *oni* everywhere, but saw nothing of the kind. No signs marked Principal Graff as anything other than a really bad role model with power over me and my friend.

Finally she said, "Now, is venting your spleen over Mr. Russel really worth risking your entire future?" She paused and split her face into a thin little smile. "I thought not. You are both dismissed."

CHAPTER TWENTY-EIGHT

No pressure tonight. When you're a heavyweight, you always wrestle last. I've heard it's different in other states, that coaches draw straws or something to choose the order of a match. In Oregon, though, you're always the anchor. Sometimes that means your match decides the whole thing. Most of the time, the 12-point spread you account for doesn't make a difference. We were winning 42–7, so I could die of a heart attack right on the mat and we'd still win. Even without Coach, we'd rolled right over the other team.

Not that I planned to lose. Mom had managed a night off, and she was sitting next to Susan in the front row. Susan and I had made up and I'd introduced them before the meet started. They were up there chatting away, a situation that scared me more than the things I'd seen in the past week.

I walked out, shook hands, waited for the whistle and pinned my guy in less than 20 seconds. Coach Vigil had told us that

Coach Russel said they had a weak team. As usual, he was right. I showered and dressed. When I got out of the locker room, I found Mom and Susan waiting together in the hall. They stood right where Susan had last time.

"Honey," Mom said, "Susan here has offered to drive you home tonight, with a detour to Shari's."

We walked her to her car. When I shut the door, she rolled open the window for a kiss goodnight. As I leaned in, she whispered, "Not Sage?"

"No," I whispered back. "Sage is just a friend."

As Susan and I walked to the student lot, she bumped her shoulder into mine. "Seriously, Connor, what's the deal with you and Sage Kaiser?"

"Good hearing," I said.

"Good enough to listen to you tell me all about you and Sage."

"Didn't we talk about that already?"

"Enough for me to be here. Not enough for me to let her live. Convince me."

"What can I say? I'm into you. I'm not into her. There's no logic to it."

"You're saying it doesn't make sense for you to be with me instead of her? That's what you're going with here?"

"No, no … wait," I stammered. I stopped. "You're messing with me."

"Maybe just a little," Susan admitted, "but still."

"I'm really trying here." I thought of saying something about how likely it was that Sage and I would be together if we wanted to, but that probably wouldn't do much good. I went with "Sage and I are buddies. I'm no more into her than I'm into Jordan or DuPree."

"So you say."

"So I mean. Okay, maybe I'm into her a little more than I'm into DuPree."

"But DuPree's seen you in your underwear. Has she ever seen you in your underwear?"

"Um," I said, dreading what had to come next. "Yes?"

"Meanie," she elbowed me in the ribs. "Now who's messing with who?"

I couldn't exactly explain the truth — that Sage had rescued me on the night of the Underwear Incident. Even if it wouldn't put Susan in danger, she'd still think I was nuts. "It's the wrestling team. Sometimes we change in tight quarters."

"Ooookay. Tell me this. Have you ever wanted to see her in her underwear?"

"No," I said immediately. I knew the right answer to this one. "No, I have not."

"Then I win," she bumped my shoulder again. This time, she stayed there long enough to take my hand.

Shari's will make you a milkshake and drop a slice of pie in it and blend the whole thing up. It tastes even better than it sounds. Susan ordered blackberry and vanilla. I went for peanut butter with chocolate. We talked about sports, mostly. Winter was her season off. She did track in the spring, multisports like a triathlon or adventure race in the summer and cross-country in the fall. I took summers off, with wrestling winter and spring, cross country in the fall. Both of us came from families without a lot of money, so we were both counting on athletic scholarships for college. I was hoping for Pacific University in Oregon, or maybe Iowa State. Susan had her eyes on University of Oregon, where the Olympic track trials are held on account of the founder of Nike inventing running shoes there once upon a time. We teased about running on the same team that September, a time that felt a long way off to me. At one point in the evening, she rubbed my leg under the table with her toes. It made my vision blurry.

Afterward, she drove me home and parked in front of my building.

"Should I walk you up?" she asked. Her voice had a kind of purr in it.

"No," I said. "If you do that, I'll have to walk you back down to the car. Then you'll walk me up again and we'll never say good night."

"That sounds kind of nice, actually." She leaned across the seat and kissed me on the lips. It was a long, warm kiss with her hands on the back of my head. She kept her mouth closed, but it was very nice all the same.

I floated out of her car and up the stairs. My hands shook and my lips felt warm. When I got inside, Mom was in her chair watching a video on the computer. She looked over her shoulder and hummed to herself.

"Mmm, mmm, mmm. I know that look."

"Huh?" I said.

"Exactly. You'll be useless all night, but you can bet I'll ask all sorts of impertinent questions at breakfast. Now off to bed with you. Mommy's watching her stories."

CHAPTER TWENTY-NINE

The bad news was that it was spirit day. Crazy Hair Friday, a day where everybody in the school shows their individuality by acting strange all at once, in the same way, when somebody in charge tells them to. Every school I'd been to had them. None had ever convinced me they were a good idea.

The good news was the spirit assembly would last the entire second half of the school day. I wasn't excited about the assembly itself, but you always had the option of going to study hall instead. Susan and I had a date to go there together. We wouldn't get to talk much, but we could sit next to each other and probably get away with passing some notes. After last night's moment, I was looking forward to that.

Carter Robinson was winding down the morning announcements when Principal Graff's voice came on the speaker.

"Ladies and gentlemen. First, I wish to congratulate all of the students at my high school for improving their attitude about trash in the cafeteria. The custodial staff tells me there is a 100 percent difference, so I have decided to lift the speaking ban effective lunch today." In other schools, a cheer might have greeted that announcement. Everyone around me just sat and waited for the other shoe to drop.

It did. "Unfortunately, several students were cited this week for breaking the ban. The following individuals will report to the cafeteria during today's spirit assembly." She read a list of about thirty names. I was on it. So were Galhardo and Fiel. Susan was not.

After lunch, we all lined up against one of the long walls in the basketball gym. I counted 33 of us. Beside me in line, Fiel and Galhardo both wore their hair teased tall and sprayed with fluorescent colors. They loved spirit days and had brought me a clown wig to put over my shaved head.

"Mom thought you'd like it," Fiel said. "We told her how you are all bald and don't have hair of your own to make crazy." I pretended to protest, but didn't fight too hard as they pulled the colorful bundle of polyester strands over my bare scalp.

Mr. Keranovak and a second janitor I didn't recognize walked to the center of the gym. Mr. Keranovak lifted a bullhorn to his lips.

"Everybody. Principal Graff has decided that you all contribute further to the final litter solution here at Ponderosa. Her words, not mine."

We all shuffled in our line. This wasn't likely to be anything but bad.

"Myself and Mr. Perez have divided you into groups of three. Each group will be responsible for picking up all the litter in a certain zone of the school grounds. Every scrap of paper. Every soda can. Every gum wrapper will be in trash bags before you go home."

A few people groaned and hissed in protest, but I kept my mouth shut. It wouldn't change things for the better and might make things worse. No point in complaining.

"It's raining pretty good out there," he continued over the noise. "If you didn't bring a rain coat, Mr. Perez will issue you a spare garbage bag. You can turn it into a poncho. It's not Beverley Hills fashion, but it should keep you dry."

Mr. Perez called out names in groups of three. To our surprise, Fiel, Galhardo and I were grouped together. Mr. Keranovak gave us our assignment: a section of trails near the back of the school grounds that is sheltered under tall cedar trees. It would be dry and, though we had a lot of ground to cover, it wasn't a high-traffic area. There wouldn't be much litter at all.

Mr. Keranovak must have seen my face as he walked past our group. He nudged me and said "A tough kid like you sometimes deserves a special break." Mr. Perez issued us our trash bags and we ran through the downpour to the shelter of the trees.

I *looked* across the school grounds as we ran and saw *oni* descending from the roof to perch on the other students out in the weather. None came our way. We were together and the surprise good treatment had left us happy. By the time we reached the trees, Fiel and Galhardo's hair dye ran in streams down their faces and into their clothes. It just made them laugh, which made me laugh. My wig even kept my scalp dry. The feelings were like demon repellant, spiritual citronella. Nothing to eat here, demons.

We'd been walking trails for a while, picking up mostly food wrappers and school papers, when Fiel looked at me sidelong and said, "So … how are things with Miss Parker?"

"Ahem. A gentleman never tells."

Galhardo stuck a candy wrapper with the point of his sword and transferred it to the garbage bag in my hand. In a singsong voice, he crooned, "That's just a gentleman's way of telling."

I pushed his shoulder, but it was a friendly shove. He pushed back. Fiel got between us, smiling. "Boys, boys. You know how I hate it when you fight."

Galhardo stopped, suddenly still. "Guys, do you hear —"

A black shape slammed into him with the force of a charging linebacker. Galhardo fell back and his sword flew into the underbrush. He landed hard on the ground with an *oni* in physical form crouching on his chest. It chittered and squealed to itself as it raised both claws to slash Galhardo's face.

Fiel darted forward and pulled his garbage bag over the *oni's* head, arms and chest. Galhardo bridged onto his neck — a wrestling technique Sage must have shown him before I came along. It popped the *oni* the rest of the way into the bag. His brother swung the bag into the nearest tree. A loud crunch and pop emanated from the bag, which collapsed like, well, like a bag full of demon that died and disintegrated.

More chittering came from the trees around us. Squinting in the gloom of the rainy winter afternoon, I could make out four more *oni* coming at us.

"The heck?" Galhardo said, gasping his way to his feet. "They're manifested. It's the middle of the day."

"They can do that?" I whispered.

"Looks like a yes," Fiel replied.

"Not good," Galhardo said, "Not good, not good."

"Whatever," Fiel growled. His face was twisted with anger at the attack on his brother. "Let's just see that none of these *oni* make that mistake again."

We were outnumbered, but Galhardo couldn't outrun the enemy here and Fiel wouldn't leave without him. We moved into a tight triangle in the middle of the path, our backs to one another, and waited for them to come.

They didn't make us wait long. The *oni* came all at once, all on Galhardo's side of our formation. He struck a fencer's pose and met the neck of the lead demon with the tip of his outstretched hand. The thing fell to the ground, clutching its throat and writhing. Fiel rolled across his brother's angled back to deliver a two-footed kick to one *oni* while snatching another by the neck.

A fourth demon leapt and landed on my face. I fell and we rolled into the bushes. It was covering my mouth and nose so I couldn't breathe, couldn't see. Its claws cut into the back of my head and dug into my shirt. I scrabbled in the mud beneath me and tried to bridge up to dislodge the monster. It held tight. I started to panic, thrashing beneath the creature as it suffocated me.

This thing was going to kill me here in the dirt, on my head like it was using the toilet. Mom would have nobody to protect her, nobody to join her for good-pizza-and-bad-movie night. The Bushido Champions would have one fewer ally to help them find the *yokai*. Susan would wind up dating other boys.

I stopped trying to breathe and focused instead on what breath I still had in front of me. Once at a lake near Bend, I had held my breath for almost two minutes, which was far more time than I'd spent struggling with this *oni*. I *looked* inside myself and found a calm center in my *dan tian* and let it expand out into my whole body. My lungs still hurt from lack of oxygen, but it wasn't worse than being out of breath. I ran my hands along the ground on either side of me until one of them found a rock.

I pulled the stone free and hit the *oni* blindly until I felt a sharp crack. The demon tried to roll away, but I rolled with it and came up straddling its chest. My breath came back to me, tearing through my throat in long, hard gasps. I pinned the *oni* and smashed it with the rock until it vanished in a puff of greasy vapor.

"Guys?" I shouted as I struggled to my feet. I was torn, filthy and terrified, but I was alive. I hoped my friends were, too. I staggered back to the trail afraid of what I might find and found them standing over the fading remains of the other three demons.

"You all right?" I panted.

"Piece of cake," Galhardo said, grinning a too-tight, too-fierce smile. "I kind of wish the bodies stuck around. We could take trophies."

"Trophies?"

"Yeah. Trophies. Like an ear or a claw. Maybe I could stuff a couple with sawdust and make a set of bookends."

"There's something very wrong with you," I said.

"Says the guy who just beat a demon to death with a rock."

I looked down at my hand. I was still holding the rock, gripping it white-knuckle tight. There was something eerie about how it had no blood on it, nothing to mark that I'd just used it in a life-or-death struggle.

"Yeah, Galhardo," said Fiel, "our man is a stone killer."

"There's nobody boulder," Galhardo said.

"Didn't you guys do rocks last time?"

"He's just taking us for granite," said Fiel.

I made myself grin, but I'm pretty sure it looked a lot like Galhardo's. "Hey, now. Fiel killed one with a trash bag."

"Technically speaking," said Fiel, "it was an emergency survival poncho."

"Still, you made him a really sad sack," I said.

Both brothers stared at me, then at each other, then back at me. Galhardo shook his head sadly.

"Don't ever do that again," Fiel said.

"Oh, no," I said. A thought had come to me in the silence of the brother's disapproval.

"What?" they said at once. They don't usually do that kind of creepy twin thing, like dressing alike or talking in unison. When they do, it's because you have their full attention.

"Alex," I said. "Sage." The demons had come for us out here. If any of us had been alone, he or she would have been toast. The others were far from our help.

"They're inside," Galhardo said. "They should be safe."

"You think so?" asked Fiel.

"Do we know?" I asked.

We were already running before I finished the sentence, down the trail and through the heavy downpour. As we crossed the inner fields, images of Sage and Alex fighting on their own rasped through my head. We sprinted through the doors and between rows of lockers, our wet feet slipping on the cheap linoleum floor. We skidded to a stop in front of the gym doors.

Inside, the big room was somber and quiet, like no spirit assembly I had ever seen. Even the lights seemed dim. *Oni* appeared when I breathed into my center and *looked*. They flew so thick I couldn't see the ceiling. Every second, a few swooped down to feast on the gloomy students below. I didn't see either of our friends, but the crowd was too thick for me to be sure.

Someone grabbed me from behind. Without thinking, I pinned an arm tight to my chest and rolled at the hips. Sage rolled over my shoulder and we both stumbled from the throw. I let go and caught myself on the wall. Fiel caught half of Sage. Alex, who must have been with her, caught the other half.

"Don't *do* that!" I gasped. I would have yelled it, but I had no wind after the scare she had given me.

"What's up with you guys?" Alex asked. Galhardo gave her a 30-second version of the fight and our run back to find them.

"My heroes," Sage grumped. She was rubbing the shoulder of the arm I'd grabbed.

"We got out of there," Alex said. "Everybody has to go up on stage one at a time. Principal Graff is complimenting their hair. Even the people who love attention are getting freaked out by the vibe. It's weird."

I looked again into the gym, feeling Galhardo and Fiel press their faces into the crack with me. A single boy stood on the stage with Principal Graff. She was talking about his hair into the microphone. I couldn't tell who it was because the stage was so thick with *oni* tearing into him.

"All finished, gentlemen?" asked a voice from behind. For the second time that afternoon I felt a rush of adrenaline and almost beat up somebody I shouldn't have. Mr. Keranovak was standing there next to Sage and Alex.

"Yes, indeed, sir," said Fiel. He was the best liar of us all. "You owe us combat pay for the condoms and tampons, though.

Mr. Keranovak raised one eyebrow.

"Seriously, that place was like the bleachers after homecoming."

"Ugh," said Alex. Mr. Keranovak looked like he was trying not to laugh.

"I don't need to go check your work, do I?"

"No, sir." Fiel fixed him with an open, honest smile. Galhardo and I avoided eye contact.

"Then it's study hall for you. I'll trust you to go straight there." He walked down the hall, whistling softly to himself. No matter how bad things got at the school, they never seemed to affect him. Maybe even a bad American high school was pretty all right compared to where he'd grown up.

I smiled. Maybe I'd get some time with Susan after all. We five walked together through halls empty of *oni* now that they were all in the gym. As we went, Fiel filled Sage and Alex in on the long version of our adventure outside.

"That *yokai* just keeps bringing more suck," Sage said. She spat out the words like she was trying to hurt them in the process of speaking.

We got to study hall, but I didn't see Susan anywhere. Maybe she'd gone to the assembly after all, since our plans to meet seemed to have fallen through. I imagined *oni* diving down on her and feasting, whispering sadness and fear and helplessness into her as she sat trapped on the cheap, plastic bleachers. A red-hot anger filled me at the thought. We had to stop the *yokai,* whomever it was.

No. We *would* stop the *yokai*. We would find it and kill it before it made things worse.

I took a chair and pretended to look at a history book while I slipped my cell phone into my lap. Susan answered my text almost immediately.

ME: Where U at?

SUSAN: Bathroom

ME: Coming back?

SUSAN: No way 2 scared

ME: I'm in study hall now

SUSAN: Might get caught and they'd put me in the gym

ME: That bad?

SUSAN: U don't know

ME: Maybe I do. Saw the assembly. Weird in there.

SUSAN: I'm staying here

ME: I'll come by your locker when it's done

SUSAN: Good. Need a hug

ME: O
SUSAN: XO
ME: XO
SUSAN: Bye.

We had to put a stop to this. That wasn't the question. The question was how we were going to find the *yokai,* and what we could do once we had.

CHAPTER THIRTY

I was winding down for bed, home alone while Mom worked another swing-and-graveyard double shift. After all the action at school, sleep was coming harder than usual. I had a major tournament in the morning with one of my old schools among the other teams.. I needed the sleep, but it just wasn't coming. After an episode of *Family Guy* on Netflix, I was about to try again when Susan popped up on my screen.

PdxSusan: Come to a party. I'll pick you up in 20.

Me: Sorry. Can't go out tonight.

PdxSusan: Let me rephrase. Come to a party _with me_. I'll pick you up in 19.

Me: Really sorry. I have a tournament tomorrow.

PdxSusan: That's tomorrow. Tonight's tonight.

Me: At 5AM.

PdxSusan: Ouch. That's freakin' early.

Me: Yes.

PdxSusan: You know, track meets start in the early afternoon.

Me: I did not know that. Sounds nice.

PdxSusan: It is nice. Lets you go to parties on Friday nights.

Me: Can I wrestle at track meets?

PdxSusan: That would be a no.

Me: Then I'll pass. Sorry about tonight, though.

PdxSusan: No prob. I can respect it. Mind if I go?

Me: Why would I mind?

PdxSusan: Sometimes boyfriends kind of mind if their girlfriends go to parties without them.

Me: Boyfriends?

PdxSusan: Yeah. Boyfriends. ☺

Me: I like the sound of that.

PdxSusan: Me, too.

Me: And no, I don't mind.

PdxSusan: When do you finish tomorrow?

Me: Around 3 or 4, but it's in Newberg. I'll be home at 7.

PdxSusan: Pick you up at the school?

Me: That would be great. I'll text you when the bus is close.

PdxSusan: OK. See you tomorrow.

Me: Bet on it. Tomorrow.

PdxSusan: XO

PdxSusan is offline.

CHAPTER THIRTY-ONE

Our team got pounded at the tournament. Coach Vigil did his best, but with our head coach gone we just didn't have the fight in us. I lost my second match on an injury timeout. The other guy had swept both my arms out when I was on all fours. With his weight on my back, I'd face planted and broken my nose. It wasn't hospital-visit broken, but bad enough that we couldn't stop the bleeding in time to finish the match. It opened again in the first round of my final match, and I had to forfeit that one, too.

I didn't even dare *look* around the bus on the way home. The way we all felt, I knew what I'd see. I felt low enough myself that the sight might open me up to an *oni,* too.

Hours later, sitting in Susan's car, my nose still hurt. My pride hurt worse. We were parked in the lot at my building after getting burgers and shakes at a drive-in.

"You can't win 'em all, champ," Susan said. She was stroking my head gently with one hand.

"Whatever," I said. I looked out my window. Cael Sanderson would disagree.

"Hey, jerk!" She smiled when she called me the name, though. "I know about losing. You're talking to a track girl."

"Track's not the same."

"I bet you it's worse."

"Riiiight," I said. This I had to hear.

"Listen. You go up against a guy every week. One on one. Two men enter, one man leaves. I get it."

"That's right. You go up against a whole heat. You can take second place and still feel good about it."

"No. No, that's not it at all. I can take first place and still feel terrible. When I run, I run against *me*. And every time I ran that race in the past. And I'll tell you, I can be pretty harsh."

I looked into her eyes and saw the truth there. She had a hard core of ambition that I knew would shine like Alex's and Sensei's if I *looked* at her just then. I really, really liked Susan, and that was part of why.

"Okay. I'd never thought of it that way before. You might have a point."

"Might? Might?" But she was smiling again. She leaned in and kissed me. It hurt my nose, but I didn't care. Susan wasn't the first girl who'd ever kissed me, but she was the first to kiss me so … thoroughly. We kissed for a long time, even though I had to keep coming up for air because I couldn't breathe through my nose. After what seemed like forever, but not nearly long enough, Susan nipped my ear and whispered, "Your mom's not home right now."

I pulled back. She was looking right into my eyes and I looked back into hers. "That's true." My voice seemed hoarse and very far away.

"Should I come up?"

"Um," I said.

Her fingers hesitated where they were stroking my chest. "That sounds like hesitation."

I took my hands off her and shook my head to clear the silky cobwebs that kept clouding my thoughts. I could hardly believe what I said next.

"Not tonight."

Susan leaned away from me. She crossed her arms and scooted back until she was leaning against her door, out of reach.

"What I mean is, um … listen. Here's how it is about me and being home alone. Mom trusts me and because she trusts me she can work this job that lets us get by without my dad around. I really, really want to take you upstairs with me. Really, really want to. But I want even more to never give Mom reason not to trust me."

Susan frowned. She still looked angry, but she nodded her head yes. She uncrossed her arms.

"There's more. She had me accidentally, and has been a single mom for a long time. She works double shifts at night because night shifts pay just a little better than day shifts, and she's so broke it makes a difference.. Her life is hard. I'm really scared of the same thing happening to me."

She nodded again, but she stayed on the other side of the car. Her eyes were hot.

"I have things I want to do with my life, Susan. So

do you. Neither of us gets to do them if we screw up and have a kid or something."

"Holy role reversal, Batman," Susan said. "You are *such* the tease. Just you wait til Tasha hears about this."

"You'd tell Tasha?"

Her eyes gleamed evilly, but she reached across and took my hand in both of hers. "That was mean of me. I'm sorry. No, I won't tell my best friend on you."

"I'm sorry, too."

"Too right you are." She scooted back in and kissed me on the cheek. "Tell you what, stud. It's okay. I can respect what you're saying, even if I'm not thrilled to hear it. I can wait for you to tell me when you're ready." She nibbled on my ear again, her breath hot on my face and the side of my neck.

Susan moved her lips from my ear to my throat, and back to my open mouth. Her lips felt very, very good there. We kissed again, just as thoroughly as before. After another forever, I pulled away to breathe and noticed blood all over her face and neck. Her eyes got wide at almost the same time.

I squeaked and pinched my thumb and finger together at the bridge of my nose. Somewhere in our make-out session, we'd reopened it. I'd bled all over both of us.

Susan had some tissues in her glove box and used them to help me pack my nose. We wiped each other off as best we could, but she'd have some explaining to do when she got home.

"It's just as well," she said as I unbuckled my seat belt and reached for the door. "I don't know if anything else would have pried me off you."

"Good night, Susan," I whispered. I forced myself through the door and into the parking lot.

"Good night, Mr. Morgan." She handed me the bundle of bloody napkins and wipes.

"Ewwwww," was all I could say.

"Hey, champ. It's your blood." She blew me a kiss and drove away. I watched her car until I could no longer see the red tail lights down the road.

"Connor," I said to myself, "what did you just do?" I hoped Coach Gable and the guys would understand.

CHAPTER THIRTY-TWO

"Ready?" Alex asked me.

"Ready," I said, and then Alex bent my arm. Skinny, pale Alex bent my arm like she was folding one of those bendy straws.

I used a rude word. "I really thought I had it that time."

"You're getting better. We'll keep practicing."

We were at the dojo for Sunday practice, working on an exercise to help us focus our chi. I was supposed to stand still and extend my arm while imagining water flowing from my *dan tian,* up my body, down my arm and out through my palm. If I did it right, it would make my arm unbendable for as long as I could stay focused. The trouble was staying focused.

Alex bent my arm again then stood still and extended her arm. It was so thin I could wrap one hand all the way around her biceps and triceps, and I pushed so hard I kept accidentally lifting her off the ground, but her elbow stayed perfectly extended.

I gave up and extended my own arm, breathed deeply and focused on my *dan tian*. I imagined it full of churning water and then I opened an imaginary valve to let that water rush up my belly and chest, through my shoulder and down my arm. I could almost see the torrent flowing out of my hand like the blast from a fire hose.

Alex pushed up on my forearm and down on my biceps. My elbow held for almost three-quarters of one breath, and then folded in half.

"What am I doing wrong?"

"Nothing." Alex gave a sideways grin as I got in position to try again. "I'm just using the same idea to make me stronger when I bend you."

"What? You're cheating?"

"I'm working ahead of the class. There's a difference."

Alex promised not to use that trick, and I was able to keep my arm straight until she distracted me by tickling my exposed armpit. At least she admitted that was cheating. We tried it a few more times each, then Sensei called us back to the center of the mat.

"You all have the first steps, the imagining of the flow of your chi. Like all things, it begins with imagining. From your imagining, you can begin to fuel changes in your body and even in the world around you until finally you can create the outcomes you require. The *oni* know this, as does the *yokai*. They use this weapon consistently. Now watch."

He called Alex to him, and she stood with her arm outstretched. Lines of concentration formed on her face as Sensei tried to bend her arm, but she kept it straight.

Then Sensei tapped one of his toes on the top of her foot and she folded up like somebody had flipped a switch.

"We can interrupt that weapon if we know how to distract their imagination and intent." He bowed to us, and we went back to practicing.

"See? I was still just working ahead of the class." Alex said. We practiced tapping, pushing, even saying the right words to distract each other and interrupt the flow of imagination, focus and chi. We were both successful about as often as we weren't.

"Good one," I said after Alex cut my focus with a combination of a kick to the shin and whispering Susan's name. "Now if we can just find a crack like that in Principal Graff's armor."

"Do you really think she's the *yokai*?" Alex asked. Having a conversation didn't make her arm easier to bend at all.

"Sage does. She really, really does, but I don't know. I mean, Mrs. Plester is dripping with *oni* these days, so she might be a candidate. Mr. Orwal's always around when something bad's happening."

"There won't be any *oni* on a *yokai*'s host. *Yokai* lash out sometimes when they're frustrated or because it amuses them. Even *oni* are smart enough to stay out of a talon's reach." Alex kept on the conversation without ever losing focus enough to let me bend her arm. She wasn't the strongest or fastest or meanest of us, but she understood chi in ways the rest of us were only beginning to.

"So, not having an *oni* on you is a sure sign of being a *yokai* … or of not being possessed at all?"

"That's about right."

"Which leaves Mr. Orwal, Principal Graff, and maybe a few others."

"How do we choose?" We both stopped. That was the big question.

Sensei called us to a halt and we gathered in a circle to bow out again. It was only my second class, but I could already say the chant along with everybody. "*Gi, Yuuki, Jin, Rei, Makoto, Meiyo, Chuugi.*" As we were about to break for the day, Alex raised her hand.

"Sensei, what do you think?

"What do I think about what, *Jin*?"

"Oh, please," Fiel said. It was the closest thing to a disrespectful tone I'd ever heard from him at the dojo. "We all heard what she and *Chuugi* were talking about. What do you think?"

Sensei sighed, but not like he was exasperated with the question or Fiel's tone. He just seemed tired. "I do not know, nor is it my place to direct you. I have too much power already, training you five. Were I to give you orders, were I to make you my private army, I doubt even the Buddha or the Christ could remain pure of intent in the face of that temptation."

"But what should we do?" Alex demanded.

"What do you feel you should do?"

"We know it's Principal Graff," Sage said. "We stop her."

"We don't know that," said Alex, "even if we think it's true."

"And if it is her, it's not really Principal Graff," said Fiel. "It's a demon wearing her body for a late Halloween costume."

"Then we stop the *yokai*. We beat it out of Principal Graff, then kill it when it shows its ugly head," Sage said.

"But we don't know for sure it's even her," said Alex.

"Am I really hearing this?" Sage was almost shouting. "Who else can it be?"

"Lots of teachers at school walk around without *oni* on them," Galhardo said.

"And how many have the access and power Graff does? How many do something that makes the whole school a little less happy every single day?"

"Mr. Orwal, for one," Alex said.

"Principal Graff's shadows act weird when you make her angry," I said. "I've never seen that with Mr. Orwal."

"First-hand experience there?" asked Fiel.

"Twice in the last two weeks," I admitted.

"My man." He held out his hand for a low five, grinning, but the joke fell flat in the angry vibe of the room.

"That's the trouble," Alex said. "What does that mean? And how do we act if we don't know? The school is getting worse every day. How long do we have until something really snaps? Until everything goes all Sandy Hook shaped?"

"Jack Cleaver already did," Sage said. Her voice was still tight.

"That's what I'm saying here," Alex said.

"Stop saying and start doing, Alex!" Sage shouted. "You know it's not just the school. If things blow up here, it's on CNN and the HuffPo. It's on YouTube. *Oni* get stronger everywhere in the world! We can't wait for you to stop stalling and move your skinny ass!"

"Hey!" Galhardo snapped, "Leave her be. She's not the problem here."

"Are you saying I am?" Sage turned on Galhardo, stalking toward the smaller boy. He had to crane his neck to keep looking at her face, but he didn't back down.

"Stop it!" I shouted. I don't usually lose my temper because my dad showed me what it could lead to. But seeing my friends arguing hurt more than breaking my nose had the day before. "This is what the *yokai* wants! If we can't stand together, we might as well serve up the whole school for dinner!"

Sage and Galhardo didn't back down, but they both looked at me instead of each other. Everything was quiet.

Sensei stood there, watching us. There was no look of judgment on his face, but he did look sad. Sad, tired and older than I'd ever seen him.

"We have to know," Alex said, "We can't attack our principal, beat her into unconsciousness, on a hunch."

Galhardo said, "Even if it worked, Mom would kill us."

"Twice," said Fiel.

"Each," said Galhardo.

Everybody laughed at the joke, but none of us really meant it. We talked more quietly after that, focusing more on solving the problem than on our uncertainty and fear. In the end, we agreed to look closely at Principal Graff for the next week and to look out for Mr.

Orwal and other possible suspects. We would make a decision at our next practice.

If we lasted that long. If the *yokai* let the school survive for another week.

CHAPTER THIRTY-THREE

Mom was already at work by the time I got home tired, discouraged and soaked from sweat and winter rain. I took a long shower that didn't seem to get me clean, and I put some finishing touches on my homework. When you're as smart as Alex or Fiel, you maybe don't have to go back and do a last check before turning stuff in. When you're only as smart as me, well, every little bit helps.

Even though I was just skimming notes and correcting worksheets, I had trouble concentrating. I kept thinking about the fight during practice, kept feeling like I used to when Mom and my dad would argue back when that was still rare. I cared about my friends at the dojo wanted them to be happy and for us to stay and work together as a team. That was something I hadn't let myself do in a long time, and the fight today made me anxious. I worried about it all night.

The worst part was how little I could do about it. Just like with Mom and my dad, the others would do whatever they were going to do. I could talk to them and maybe some of them would listen to some of what I said, but that was all.

It scared me. I could lose this thing, just like I'd lost so many other things, and I couldn't blame it on moving away this time. I was powerless to make any real difference; I could only watch what happened.

I felt sad. My nose hurt. I didn't know what to do. Even my posters on the wall had no advice for me that night.

There was a knock at the door. I almost fell out of my chair as a rush of adrenaline chased away the stupor I'd worked myself into. Wishing I had some kind of weapon, I crept to my door and looked through the peephole.

Susan was there, her arms crossed over a loose triathlon sweatshirt. Her eyes looked red even through the fisheye lens. Her hair was wet from the misting rain. I opened the door.

"Hey, Susan. I didn't expect to see you tonight." She turned her head as I leaned in for a kiss. I got a face full of hair.

"Yeah, well. I dropped by earlier but you were busy. Was that Sage's car I saw picking you up?"

Uh, oh. You might have noticed by now that I'm not very good with women, but even I knew to step very carefully into a conversation like that. Trouble was, I didn't know where to step. I tried the truth. "Um, yes. She took me to practice because of the rain."

"Wrestling practice?"

"Um, no."

"That other practice?"

"Um, yes."

"The one you and she do together, but you won't tell me about?"

"Um, yes?"

"The one you go to with the girl I caught you grinding against on your locker?"

"Um, it wasn't my —"

"Your locker? That's what you're going with here, that it wasn't your locker you were grinding against her on?"

"We weren't —"

"Don't you tell me I didn't see what I saw!" She was yelling now, exploding at me.

"But it wasn't what you think!" I raised my own voice. Even in the middle of things, a part of me knew it was a bad idea. It was just so unfair. I'd never cheat on her with anybody, least of all Sage. She was accusing me unjustly and I'd had enough unfairness for one day.

"Don't you shout at me, Connor. I came by to make up and now you're shouting?" Her face was getting as red as her eyes. Even in the rain, her voice echoed off the buildings on the other side of the parking lot.

"I'm not yelling," I yelled.

"Yes you are," she yelled back.

The argument had reached the point where we were yelling at each other about whether or not we were yelling. If you've never been in a relationship, there's no way to make that make sense. I shut up. Nothing I said at that point would do either of us any good.

Susan shut up, too. She opened her mouth, closed it again. She spun around and stomped down the stairs.

I opened my mouth, couldn't think of anything to say, and closed it. I stepped out onto the walkway, but I didn't chase her down the stairs. Her car sped away, the tires squealing on the wet pavement. I stood there alone in the rain, even sadder than I'd been before.

"Is okay," said a voice from below. I looked down to see Mrs. Dochevnya looking at me through the gaps in the walkway boards. "Strong girl is good girl, but very also is loud girl also. She will listen when her mind again grows quiet."

I just closed my door. I wasn't in the mood.

I grumbled to myself as I finished my homework. Every few seconds, I'd look at my computer to see if Susan had logged in. She never did, or if she did she blocked me so I couldn't see her. That was most likely. If she did it that way, she could gripe to all her friends without me there to tell my side. I could just imagine what Tasha would have to say. Once again, I was on the outside. Excluded. Alone.

At 10:00 I loaded my backpack for the morning and slumped into bed. I turned my head to Coach, Kyle and Cael. "Seriously, guys. What do I do now?"

Got me, said Coach.

No idea, said Kyle.

We were hoping you'd know, said Cael.

But we're eager to see how it turns out, said Kyle.

"Thanks guys. Thanks a lot." I turned out the lights and lay there for a long time before I finally fell asleep.

CHAPTER THIRTY-FOUR

I dreamed of a night when I was nine years old. My dad had been gone for three straight days then stumbled through the back door just before dinner. His shirt was missing and he stank of vomit, beer and meth. He might have had a new tattoo, but I'd never kept close enough track to be sure.

Mom tried to hug him, but he pushed her away hard enough to make her fall on her bottom. She cussed. Even I could tell it was from the pain, but my dad thought she was cussing at him. He charged at her, roaring like, well, like my dad would roar when he was drunk and high and angry.

She scooted away on her bottom and turned to scramble away on all fours. My dad, still impaired from days of partying, stumbled and tripped over the cheap living room furniture. He fell onto and through one of our wooden kitchen chairs, breaking it into a pile of sticks.

By the time he caught Mom by the ankle, he was as angry as I'd ever seen him. His chest heaved and sweat dripped from his hair. He grabbed her with one hand and used the other to slap her back and forth across the face. Mom held her arms up to block the blows, but her head still whipped around with each slap.

I don't know exactly when I grabbed the broken-off chair leg, but suddenly I was running across the room holding it in both hands. I hit my dad across the backs of both legs as hard as I could. He fell to his knees. For a second, he stopped hitting Mom.

Then he backhanded me across the chest. I tumbled backward across the room and landed against our Goodwill-store coffee table. My dad picked Mom up with one arm and held her upright. He closed his fist and hit her like a punching bag. Every third or fourth punch, he glared at me to make sure I was still watching.

I lay there, staring. I tried closing my eyes, but the sounds of it were worse than seeing what he was actually doing to her. He hit her and hit her until she went so limp he couldn't hold her up anymore, and then he dropped her to the ground and went at her with his feet. He kicked her again and again and again and again ...

I woke up. I was breathing fast and covered in a cold sweat. My blanket lay in a bundle on the floor and my sheets were twisted around my legs. I sat up and breathed myself back into the present.

That night had been seven years ago. I was too weak to help Mom then, and she still had scars from it. Physical and emotional. I had my own wounds from that night, too, but they couldn't be as bad as hers.

I walked to the bathroom, still sweating, past posters of heroes who had nothing to say. We'd talked about it plenty of times before, and there was nothing new to add. I splashed my face and looked in the mirror. My eyes were bright red, like Susan's had been earlier. I'd been crying in my sleep.

The years since had made me bigger and wrestling had made me stronger. I was an athlete now, maybe even a warrior, if I understood what that word really meant. I hadn't been able to do anything for Mom that night, but today I could.

And I would. Maybe not for Mom this time, but I was strong enough to help my friends and my school. Who knew? If the *oni* really were everywhere I could do my part to save the whole world.

I felt something almost like movement in my *dan tian* and I focused my awareness on it. There was energy there, power, that was different from in class earlier that day. The water was boiling now, with angry heat from the memory of what I hadn't been able to stop my father from doing. When I let the steam from that heat flow through me, I felt stronger than I ever had before in my life.

Mom had said they were putting my dad away for three years, which was long enough to get better if he decided he wanted that for himself. Maybe he would. Maybe he wouldn't. Either way, I'd be three years bigger and three years stronger by then. I'd have to pay him a visit. We could have a brief, but meaningful, talk about that night. I was sure I could communicate my point of view.

In the meantime, I could use my strength to keep what I had. I liked being part of the Bushido Champions.

I liked having Mrs. Dochevnya in the apartment downstairs. I liked Ponderosa, and I liked Susan.

The *oni* would not take that away from me. I wouldn't let them.

I bumped fists with myself in the mirror, drank some water and climbed back into bed.

CHAPTER THIRTY-FIVE

Monday morning started out all right. Mom wasn't working. Instead of going to bed like she should have, she stayed up to make sourdough French toast. My favorite. The Portland winter rain broke just long enough for me to stay dry all the way to school. My bike lock even shut on the first try.

Things went downhill from there.

I walked by Susan three times in the hall before classes started. She had her hair and face done up like a first date and wore snug running tights and a shirt that clung tight to her top half. She looked beautiful, sexy, but she didn't look at me. Every time I approached, she turned her back on me just slowly enough to let me know she was doing it on purpose. That just left Tasha to smirk at me as I slunk away.

English class was a test for the whole period. I rushed through it then slid my cell phone out of my pocket.

ME: Listen. Can we talk?

Nothing at all for five minutes. It felt like five hours.

ME: Really. Let's talk about this.

Nothing for another six minutes.

ME: What can I say?

Three minutes and forty seconds later — I was watching the second hand of the wall clock make its circles by then — Susan responded.

SUSAN: Say it later. I'm not talking to you.

SUSAN: Jerk.

I felt last night's sadness creeping over me again. Was this the last straw of an already tough beginning? I liked Susan. A lot. I liked me and Susan even more. We were really only starting to date, but it felt like something that could be real. Like the sort of thing Mom watched in her romantic comedies.

I tried converting the sadness to a sense of purpose the way I would with physical pain on the mat, the way I had with the dream, but I couldn't find the boiling hot energy in my *dan tian* like I had the night before.

The clock said four and a half minutes since her last text. It was going to be a rough morning. Whenever we were in the same room together, she made a point of looking at everything and everybody but me. She even talked to guys she'd never seemed interested in before. Things went pretty much that well for the rest of the day. The only bright spot was when Tasha poked me as I was heading down the hall for the locker room.

"Hang in, tough guy," she said. "Fat lady hasn't sung yet."

And then it was time for practice.

CHAPTER THIRTY-SIX

My name was on the challenge board again. So was DuPree's. We were the only match up there for the day. That late in the season most of the team knew their places, but DuPree had a different attitude. He considered the varsity slot his territory. As far as he was concerned, I was just borrowing it until he felt like taking it back. Sage and I rolled together through practice, and then it was time to go.

Round one went like it usually did between us, with DuPree and me chasing each other for takedowns. We each got one, and I escaped once. The round ended with me ahead, 3–2. He took up position for the second round. Most of it was a fight with me trying to get up and DuPree holding on for dear life. I got loose in the last few seconds, but he flew at me with a football tackle while I was still catching my balance from the escape. He turned it into a takedown as the whistle blew.

I chose both of us standing for round three, with the score tied at four points each. When the round started, DuPree charged up and caught me in a clinch. No matter where I went, he held me there. He cranked on my neck and pushed my head toward the floor, forcing me to focus on balance and position instead of moving so I could wear him out and take advantage of my superior wind. DuPree held me in place and ran down the clock. About a minute in, Coach broke us apart and cautioned him for stalling. When he started the action back up, DuPree charged in and clinched me again. This time, he whispered in my ear.

"A little trouble on the home front this weekend? You and Susan on the outs?"

I smacked the side of my head into his temple in a short head-butt. That's not technically legal, but it happens all the time. If nobody bleeds, the refs almost never call you on it. Neither did Coach. "Screw you, DuPree."

"Good idea. Maybe that's why she asked me over tonight."

I blinked. In that moment, DuPree dropped to both knees and slid one arm between my legs. He tossed me to the ground in a fireman's carry and laid me flat on my back. He spun and grabbed my head and one leg. I was stuck, with most of a minute left in the match. There was nobody to fight for this time, and even if I got free I'd be down by five points. No way could I make that up in the time remaining. There was no point to it.

All the fight left me. I let him roll me on my back and waited for Coach Vigil to slap the mat.

Which he did.

I changed without talking to anybody, stalked out to the bike rack, struggled with my lock, hopped on and rode home. It was raining again. Mom wasn't there, so I microwaved the last of the French toast and fiddled around with YouTube videos. None of them seemed as funny as they promised to be. In another window, a message from Susan popped up.

PdxSusan: Tough break. UOK?

I ignored her.

PdxSusan: Hey, I'm ready to talk if you are.

I logged out. *Connor Morgan is offline.* See how she liked it.

My phone rang twice, once from Mom and once from Susan, before I turned it off. I threw my clothes in a corner and got under the covers in my underwear. My mind was spinning. Susan might be hooking up with DuPree any minute, maybe even right then. Maybe they'd been together when Susan tried to message me. With DuPree, of all people. The one person in the school she had to know would hurt me the most.

Maybe she'd been with him from the beginning, from that first night DuPree and Arturo and Ivan had chased me. Maybe she'd gotten my attention just so she could tell them where I was. The whole thing was just an elaborate revenge plot for my taking his place on the team. And I'd walked right into it like the world's biggest sucker.

It figured. Just last night, I'd been thinking about how much I liked this place, about permanence and connection and belonging. Now I knew better. Attachment just meant vulnerability and blindness, nothing more.

When I finally did fall asleep, I dreamed of walking on an ice-covered lake. I kept breaking through and Susan kept not saving me.

CHAPTER THIRTY-SEVEN

Mom was out when I woke up, working another double shift. She did that a lot because of the stupid nursing shortage and our stupid single-parent household. I got ready alone and biked to school, pedaling hard and moving fast.

Susan was with DuPree out on the bus ramp. She faced him, standing way too close. I could see from 10 feet away that her face was red, like when she first kissed me in the parking lot.

It was true. Suddenly, I knew it. I knew it like I knew my father was a deadbeat drug addict who would never get his life on track. Like I knew Mom resented me for making her life so hard since they split up. I *knew.*

The well of energy in my *dan tian* boiled like it had the other night after my dream. The steaming power expanded to fill my stomach, my chest, every limb in my body. It practically carried me across the concrete toward where the two of them stood.

Kids around us stared. Trust the herd at a high school to tune in when it looked like there might be some free drama. DuPree saw me first. He stood up straight. Susan turned to face me. She blushed even brighter. Over her head, DuPree smirked. He winked at me with his left eye.

The energy boiling inside me made it impossible for me to talk. I could only look at Susan and try not to cry.

"Connor," her voice was small and weak, like not even she believed what she was saying. "It isn't true."

"Liar!" the word came out of my mouth with the force and speed of a punch.

She cried little crocodile tears. "Connor, you can't believe —"

"What I can't believe is you think I'm stupid enough to listen to your lies. Look at your face! You're blushing!

"I'm not blushing! I'm angry!"

"Don't talk to me about angry! Just get the hell away from me!"

"Connor, I —"

"Are you going deaf? Shut up! Go! Away!"

Susan opened her mouth and started to wail. Tasha came out of the crowd and gathered her in her arms. She shot me a blistering look that I ignored. If Susan didn't care about me, why should I care about her friends?

I turned to DuPree and took the last step between us. He just looked at me, still wearing that smirk. My *dan tian* boiled even hotter, so hot that I had to work to keep the steam from pushing my fist directly into his mouth. He'd taken my spot on the team. He'd taken my girlfriend, if she'd even been mine to begin with. My hands tightened at my sides, but I forced myself to open them. I turned around and walked away, even though a part of me screamed *Coward!* with every step.

Behind me DuPree called out, "Too bad, Morgan! Better luck next time!"

It was like watching myself from outside my body. I saw myself turn and run at DuPree, tackling him around the waist. He fell hard onto the concrete of the bus ramp and I straddled him where he lay. I punched his stupid, fat face one, two, three, four times before people I didn't even know pulled me off him and pushed me away.

DuPree got up, holding his nose. Blood dripped out below his hand, down his chin and onto the pavement.

"You psycho!" he shouted. "I never touched her! I was just messing with your head to get my spot!"

"Shut up!" I shouted back. "Shut the hell up!" I found my bike, got on it, rode the hell away from school.

I pumped my legs as fast as they could go, using the still-boiling center of energy in my *dan tien*. I wondered why Sensei never showed us how to use it like this, there was so much power there. I couldn't believe Susan had the gall to lie right to my face. She been standing right next to him, up close, the way she would with me after we'd started going out.

It was my fault. She'd made it clear on Saturday night what she wanted, but I said no out of a stupid, babyish need to make my mommy happy. I was such a coward when things mattered. So she let DuPree take care of her needs, and she let him use that to beat me in the challenge match. It was probably even her idea. They'd probably been together before I even came to Ponderosa. I bet everyone in the school knew all about it. Everybody was against me, and they had all come out this morning to watch the final act of the play. No matter where I went, no matter how many times I moved, there was never any place for me to belong. Never.

I got home and watched Netflix while I ate a whole box of Captain Crunch by hand. It hurt the top of my mouth the same way the stupid teen drama on the screen hurt my brain. I didn't even log on to Facebook.

My phone rang. It was Susan. I ignored it. It rang again and again. Eventually she gave up. I deleted the voice mail and texts without opening any of them. Somehow, I found the energy to drag my ass to bed. I collapsed on top and lay there, still thinking about DuPree and Susan and how I was going to get my revenge.

I had to make them pay, would make them pay. They'd regret what they'd done just as soon as I came up with a good enough plan. I was still thinking about it when Mom came home from work. She called my name a bunch of times, then knocked and cracked my door open. She said my name again. I pretended to be asleep. After a while, she turned off my light and shut the door.

That night, I dreamed of drowning DuPree in a frozen lake. I dreamed of watching the ice break beneath him and Susan, and not saving them even when they begged for help.

CHAPTER THIRTY-EIGHT

It was still dark outside when Mom turned on my light. She dragged a kitchen chair into my room and sat next to my head. She shook me.

"Connor, honey, are you awake?"

I creaked one eye open and glared at her. "Do I *look* awake?"

"I got a strange call last night during my shift. From your principal."

I sat up, crossing my arms across my chest. I stared at her without saying anything. If she wanted me to feel bad about punching DuPree in the head, she was going to have to work for it.

"Do you want to tell me about it?"

"Why? I thought you said Principal Graff already did."

"She said you got in a fight and then skipped school."

"He had it coming," I said. I made the words a growl.

"How?"

"It's personal."

"Come on, Connor. Tell your mom?

"It's personal, Mother. As in, I keep it to my own personal self."

"I'm afraid that won't do, young man. You're in serious trouble at school. If you want my help, you're going to have to —"

"I don't remember asking you for any damn help." I wasn't exactly yelling, but I could feel the tone and tension rising in my voice. That boiling power in my *dan tian* was back and fueling me for the fight.

"Connor Ireaia Morgan, just who do you think you're speaking to? You're not acting like yourself this morning. Are you using drugs?"

"No!" Now I was yelling, screaming, the power pushing me to my feet so I loomed over my mother, bending down to put my face right in front of hers. She flinched away, like she used to with my dad, but she didn't back off.

"I'm not using drugs!" I waved my arms and she flinched back in the little chair. "Not one time! Not even beer! You leave me here alone three nights, four nights in a week. There's always beer in the fridge. Has there ever been even one bottle missing?"

I stood over her, panting with the effort of not hitting the smaller, weaker woman cowering in front of me. She whined up from where she sat, "Connor, I didn't realize."

"Of course you didn't realize! You're never around to realize a damned thing!" I grabbed my shoes off the floor and threw them on without tying the laces. Mom followed me to the door, but I was faster than her and slammed it in her face behind me. I was down the stairs and on my bike before she got it open again. Mom stood in the doorway and hollered at me. She sounded like she was crying.

Not that I cared.

If she really loved me, she would have come down the damn stairs. I wheeled out of there, almost running over Mrs. Dochevnya where she stood on the pavement in front of her door. She jumped out of the way at the last minute.

That's right. Best get out of my way today. Everybody had best just get out of my way.

Get the hell out of my way.

I didn't ride to school. There was nothing there for me. My varsity spot was gone, and I was probably off the team completely for kicking DuPree's ass. Susan wasn't my girlfriend anymore, probably never was. The Bushido Champions were a sad joke. The whole damn school, the whole damn world, was full of demons and what were they doing about it? Playing secret soldiers and rolling around together once a week. Like the Mickey Mouse club in dumber pajamas. They couldn't even figure out who the bad guy really was.

I ended up at Waterfront Park, by the river, riding past street people sleeping under benches. Most of them went south for the winter like sad, ragged birds, but a few huddled under cardboard boxes to keep out the seeping rain. It seemed like half of them had a mangy, hungry-looking dog with a piece of clothesline for a leash.

That was probably where I was headed. Everything I tried was too little, too late. Sure, I'd enjoy some temporary time in the sun. I'd have a few matches on the varsity team, a couple of dates with Susan, but I would always fail in the end. If I weren't screwing it up, Mom would always move us just when things were going good. I would never have a real chance to make it to the top of anything.

I never should have come to Ponderosa at all. Mom should never have moved us up from Eugene. She never should have left my dad and sure as hell never should have had me. I was a burden to her, the reason she and my dad split up. Without me, his drugs would have been a habit, not a problem. It was only the extra responsibility of having a loser kid that made Mom walk out.

Without me around, they could get back together. Mom wouldn't have to come home from Eugene crying every few months. Eugene could be home again without me. Kids wouldn't have somebody to laugh at anymore if I weren't around. I wouldn't have to deal with all this too-much-for-me crap that was going on.

I braked my bike to miss one of those mangy street dogs, lost traction, skidded sideways and went into a low slide. My helmeted head cracked on the sidewalk and I rolled to a stop. I lay on the ground, my head spinning, the rain splashing down on my face.

Mom would be better off without me, I thought as I lay on the wet ground hurting from the fall. My dad would, too. Everybody, even me, would be happier if I weren't around anymore. The wet soaked into me as I lay still, thinking about that simple fact and how important it was. Nobody came to see if I was all right.

Mom had a gun in her closet. A revolver. She didn't know I knew, but I saw her cleaning it once. I guessed she had it to protect her from my dad or his friends, back when we were still in Eugene and he'd have to get violent because he still loved her and I was keeping them apart.

She had a gun in her closet.

It was really that simple.

She had a gun in her closet. And bullets. I'd never fired one, but it couldn't be that hard. Gangbangers do it all the time, and they're about as smart as wet paint.

I rolled to my knees, still a little dizzy, and crawled through the mud to my bike. I levered myself up, got on and pumped my legs through the long route home. The rain stung my face.

The solution was simple, obvious to anybody not as stupid as I was. I didn't know why I hadn't thought of it years before. Everybody would be better off. Especially me, especially Mom. The only question was if I would just do myself or if I would take Susan and DuPree with me.

CHAPTER THIRTY-NINE

I'd ridden farther than I thought before my crash and pedaled back in a daze. The lights and trees and grass and buildings seemed separate from me, like I was watching the world through a window. By the time I got back to the apartments, it was fully dark. Soaked clear to my underwear from the misting rain, I pulled up and dropped my bike on the asphalt. I didn't bother to lock it. In a few minutes, it wouldn't matter.

Mom was working another double shift, so I knew she'd be gone. She was never home when it really counted. She couldn't talk me out of my decision, but it would have been nice to be able to explain myself. I was sure she'd agree in time. She'd cry a little, maybe, but then she'd admit she had always wished for me to be gone, that she'd never really wanted me in the first place.

It would be a late Christmas present for her. She and my dad could even celebrate on Valentine's Day. It would have to be in a prison visiting room, but that was just another misery of Mom's that was my fault. He'd be out some day, and they could be together then.

I had one foot on the stairs when a door opened behind me. Mrs. Dochevnya's voice called out to me. "Strange boy." I ignored her.

Before I could take a step, a strong hand grabbed my elbow and spun me around so hard I almost fell from the force. Mrs. Dochevnya stood in front of me, looking up at my rain-slicked face. "Strange boy, what are you doing?"

"Whatever it is, old woman, it's none of your business." I turned back toward the stairs. Mom's gun was right up there. I could be done with this in less time than it would take to check my email. Susan and DuPree wouldn't be coming with me that way, but you can't have everything.

"Look at me, strange boy," Mrs. Dochevnya was still holding on to my elbow. I reached for the powerful rage that had been boiling all day inside me, but for some reason I couldn't make it flow. I felt sad and weak, not angry and strong. The old woman peered at me from the middle of her wrinkled, mustached face.

"Screw you!" I shouted. I tried to pull my arm away, but it wouldn't budge.

"You shout at me?" she said. Her voice stayed calm, but strong. She didn't seem afraid, being yelled at by a teenager twice her size. She didn't flinch like Mom had. Her expression never changed. "I heard you shouting at your mother. I heard you then and I hear you now, and I say to myself, I think this is not the strange, nice boy who I know."

"What do you know?" I shouted back. "What do you know about anything?"

"I know what happened yesterday, what happened this morning. Your crying mother told me. Told me how you roared like lion and ran like mouse."

"I thought you said I ran like a rabbit." The stupid crone couldn't even keep her animals straight.

"Not today, strange boy. Today you ran like mouse. Rabbits are smart, not stupid."

"Are you calling me stupid, old hag?"

"Are you acting stupid, strange boy?"

"Let me go!" I tried to pull my arm away, but somehow she was still too strong.

"No," she said. I pulled my arm harder. She didn't let go. "No," she said again.

I balled the hand of my free arm into a fist. If she wouldn't let go, I'd make her let go. Punching people out was just going to be part of how I rolled for what was left of my miserable life.

My shin exploded with pain. Immediately I realized Mrs. Dochevnya had slammed it with the tip of her hickory cane. I hopped on the other leg as I bent to clutch my shin with my free hand. Mrs. Dochevnya slapped me on the back of the head.

It wasn't a little dope slap like Mom sometimes gave me when I had it coming. Mrs. Dochevnya had strong arms and a hand as hard as a wooden plank. It knocked me to my knees and darkened the edges of my vision. I wanted to pass out.

Mrs. Dochevnya wouldn't let me. She grabbed me by the jaw with her free hand and bent close to my face.

She looked deep into my eyes until I felt she was reading the most private thoughts in the back of my brain. She spoke, very quickly, in her own language. I couldn't understand the words, but it sounded like swearing. A lot. And meaning it. She finished with something like *bazmoiti miti!*

Suddenly I felt very tired. I wanted to fall the rest of the way down, but Mrs. Dochevnya still held me upright. Something cold tickled my ear, and I saw an oily shadow drop onto my shoulder and take shape. I leaped back just as Mrs. Dochevnya stabbed with her cane to pin the *oni* against the cinder-block wall of our building. It squirmed there, in physical form, hissing and spitting. She just looked at it the way she might have looked at something a dog had left on her doormat.

She said to the *oni,* in English, "You will not hurt the strange boy anymore."

It squeaked up at her, "You haven't won! This is only the beginning. We are legion, serving the master! Your young protectors will fall one by one. All you can do is despair!"

"That may be, sad little shadow. But *you* will not hurt the strange boy anymore." She pulled a salt shaker out of her bathrobe and unscrewed the cap with one hand. She sliced it across the air, loosing an arc of the white grains through the air. Where it landed on the *oni,* it smoked. The shadowy body bubbled as if it were being eaten by acid. It screamed one more curse then dissipated into the dark night air.

Mrs. Dochevnya helped me up the stairs. I was so weak I could barely stand. She borrowed my keys to unlock the door then led me to my bedroom. She started to help me undress. When I tried to fight, she said, "Strange boy, I have changed many children in my life. Some were even older than you." I gave up and let her help me into a pair of sweats I'd left on the floor Monday night. She tucked me in then walked softly out of my room.

I heard the front door close and the lock turn from the inside. Out in the living room, Mrs. Dochevnya began singing a lullaby in a language I didn't understand, but I knew it was about being protected, warm and safe.

I fell asleep and did not dream.

CHAPTER FORTY

"Mr. Connor Morgan," Principal Graff said. She stood behind her desk, looking down her nose at me. Fluorescent ceiling lights threw her shadow on the wall behind her. It looked normal for the moment, but still I watched it carefully. I'd spent three days distracted from our fight against the Yokai, and I wanted to make up for the lost time. Mom was sitting next to me, both of us in the hard, wooden visitor chairs.

Graff continued, "Do you have anything to say for yourself?"

Mrs. Dochevnya had stayed until Mom came home, and we all talked. Talked and cried a little and hugged a lot. Both of us said we were sorry even though I was the only one who'd done anything wrong. I told her it would never happen again. She said she'd love me even if it did. She seemed to think it was some kind of hormone thing.

Even without that drama, it had been a long morning. Mr. Orwal had been waiting for me by the front door and escorted us both to the front office. Mom and I waited for more than an hour before Principal Graff called us in. Even then, she had taken her time. Mom had to call in late to work. Twice.

I cleared my throat. What *did* I have to say for myself? "Just that I'm sorry. I don't know what came over me. I wasn't myself." That wasn't strictly true, but explaining what really happened wouldn't help anybody. "It won't happen again."

Those were close to the exact words I'd used with Mom, but when you screw up as badly as I had, there are only so many things to say.

"Mrs. Morgan, do you have anything to add?"

Mom was smiling. It was the shiny smile she got when she talked to patients who were being unreasonable. A smile that said she was being polite because that was her job even if she really, really wanted to test her brand-new rectal thermometer on you the hard way.

Her words.

She said, "No."

Principal Graff looked disappointed. Her shadow swayed slightly as if it had been blown by the wind. She inhaled, a long breath in through her nose that implied endless patience in the face of deep disappointment. She said, "In light of your … history … with Mr. Dupree, the altercation last Tuesday was perhaps understandable. Deplorable, but understandable. Boys will, after all, be boys.

She shot me a condescending glance then looked at Mom over the rims of her glasses. Neither of us responded.

"Understandable as it may be, your actions cannot be

overlooked. And, of course, skipping two days of school can never pass without formidable consequences."

I did my best to look frightened. I really did, but mostly I was trying not to laugh. The punishment, whatever she had in mind, would hurt. It should hurt. I had it coming. But all of her verbal gymnastics wouldn't make it hurt worse. Principal Graff might be dangerous at other times, in other ways, but at the moment she was mostly just silly.

"In other schools you have attended, you may have noticed that they punish skipping school with a day of suspension. Personally, I find this ridiculous. It's like handing the child a buy one, get one free coupon for misbehavior. Here at Ponderosa, we go the opposite direction. For each day you skipped, you will serve one day of in-school suspension. You will receive no credit for any assignments due or given out on any of the four days you miss class."

Mom broke in. "I would like to connect with his teachers. He may not get credit for it, but he will complete every assignment at home."

"Quite," Principal Graff said. You could tell by her tone that she didn't like the interruption. The room seemed to grow a shade darker and her shadow loomed. "I shouldn't be surprised, Mr. Morgan, if your eligibility to compete on the wrestling team were compromised by this."

I was getting mostly Bs and even a few As. Even if the suspension cost me a full letter grade in every class, I was in no danger of falling below the 2.0 grade-point average required to compete. Still, I grimaced.

The suspension alone could cost me a week or two of competition. DuPree would use the time to get entrenched in his spot, maybe even long enough to bump me out of regional competition at the end of the regular season.

"Mrs. Morgan, thank you for your time. I know it was a hardship for you to miss work because of your son's mistakes."

"No problem," Mom said, still smiling. "What happens now?"

"At other schools, students suspended in school sit in a study hall. Since they have no relevant homework, they generally spend that time reading popular fiction or drawing on their desks with permanent markers. At Ponderosa, we find good use for the time and energy of students in this situation."

"And what, exactly, will he be doing?"

Principal Graff looked startled by the question. Maybe she wasn't used to being asked that kind of thing. "I would have to check with Mr. Keranovak, our chief custodian, but I believe he plans to move several tons of fertilizer for our horticulture department. Mr. Morgan will assist his staff in that effort."

"I don't know if I can go along with that, Miz Graff."

The room got two shades darker and noticeably chillier. I filed that information away for future reference, but at that moment getting Mom out and back to work was my biggest priority. She got paid by the hour.

"It's all right, Mom," I said. "It's a little weird, but I'll get a good workout from shoveling fertilizer all day. I'm going to miss three practices and a meet. I need it."

I looked at her eyes. I could tell she wanted to fight, but I just wanted this to be over. Besides, I liked Mr. Keranovak. It probably wouldn't be that bad. "It'll be okay. Please?"

"If you say so," Mom said, putting the emphasis on *you*. She shook Principal Graff's hand formally then hugged me goodbye.

"See you late tonight, Connor. Maybe tomorrow morning." She would have to work a double to make up for the time she'd lost.

"See you, Mom. Love you."

"Love you, too."

Mom left. I turned back to Principal Graff, who looked scandalized by our open display of affection. I wondered if she had a husband or kids of her own, anybody to say they loved her in the middle of a hard day. If not, maybe that had made her an easier target for control by a *yokai*.

"What now?" I said.

"Officer Orwal will escort you to your work assignment." She pushed some buttons on her phone. A moment later, the security chief showed up at the door. He led me out of the office and through the halls toward the back of the school. As we walked, I heard the whispers and saw the looks of my classmates all around. It was just like Principal Graff to choose a passing period for my perp walk. Some kids I didn't know well even pointed as I went by. At least I didn't see DuPree or Susan. As I passed the drinking fountains by the large gym, Sage threw a wad of paper at me. It hit me in the ear harder than you'd think somebody could throw something that light.

"I love you, too, *Gi*." I shouted over my shoulder. Mr. Orwal scowled.

It turned out I wouldn't get to work with Mr. Keranovak that morning since he worked the swing shift and wouldn't be in until 2:00 in the afternoon. I was with Mr. Torres, a short, bald man from Columbia. Some movies make fun of Latin accents, but his was so thick he sounded like he was making fun of those movies.

He led me to the school's loading dock, a wide space behind the cafeteria. On one side, a stack of maybe 200 bags of fertilizer stood on wooden pallets. Using mostly hand signals, Mr. Torres let me know I was going to carry them, by hand, to the horticulture buildings on the far side of the running track. It was a little more than 100 yards each way. He led me to a recently cleared patch of concrete where I was supposed to stack them and then left me to my work.

It was harder and took longer than I'd expected, but at least it wasn't raining and I never got overheated in the January chill. I focused on the feel of my muscles as they lifted the heavy bags, enjoying how easy it was and how strong that easiness made me feel. I might not get to wrestle against anybody for the next few days, but I kicked those bags' butts all over the place. Physical effort has always helped me feel calm and centered. It occupies just enough of my brain to turn off that constant back-of-the-mind static that can dominate you with fear and doubt if you let it.

As I moved, that calm feeling settled in my *dan tien*. I felt it swell and grow inside me, a warm and cool sensation nothing like the boiling rage that had been there for the past few days. I let it expand to fill my limbs and chest, and the 70-pound bags felt even lighter.

Not many students spent time out by the horticulture buildings, so I didn't have to deal with that kind of drama. Only one class met during the day, with just 10 kids attending. Fiel was one of them. He snuck me a thumbs-up sign when the teacher had his back turned.

Mr. Orwal came to take me to the office for lunch. By then, I'd lugged about 60 of the bags. He looked impressed at the pile I'd managed to stack so far. We went back through the halls, this time before the passing period. I ate my sack lunch in one of the Chairs of Shame.

I had just finished my last grape when Coach Russel came in. I'd been so distracted with my own stuff, I hadn't heard about his reinstatement. He jabbed a finger at me, then at the empty nurse's office. I sat on the patient bed, with him on the rolling doctor stool. He shut the door.

Coach looked at me, held my eyes for what felt like half an hour. "Are you all right?" he said at last.

"Um, yeah, Coach. I miss practice, but I'm okay. What about you?"

"I'm fine, young man. Thank you for asking. But I'm not important right now."

"Really, Coach. I heard what happened. It was wrong."

Coach took a deep breath and let it out through his nose. He said, "Sometimes things happen that aren't fair. Sometimes they happen and there's nothing you can do about it just then. Sometimes there's nothing you can do, ever. When that happens, you take it like a man and focus on what's important."

I nodded. We were quiet for a moment, together.

"Connor, you're important. This wasn't like you. Missing practice. Skipping school. It's not who you are."

"I know, Coach. Mom thinks I had some kind of hormone attack."

"Do you think she's right?"

I didn't think anything. I knew what had happened. I owed Coach my respect, but the truth put him in danger of attack. Coach Russel possessed by an *oni* was too scary to think about. "I think I wasn't myself for a few days. I'm better now, and I think I know how to stay out of that head space."

Coach chewed his lip for a few seconds and said, "A story came to my attention yesterday. Morgan, it was rookie of you to let DuPree get in your head like that."

"Yes, Coach. I know."

"You're off the varsity squad for this week, banned from competition. You can't come watch. But you'd lost your spot to DuPree, anyway. It's one of the things that started this whole mess, I'll bet. You can't challenge on your first day back, so you're off for next week, too. Do you know what pisses me off the most about this?"

I knew better than to answer.

"You're better than him. You're a better wrestler and a better person. And between the early season and these two weeks, I don't know which one of you will have the better record come time to choose our team for the regionals." He spoke in a calm, even sad voice. It was worse than when he swore. "You're only a sophomore, but people on the team look up to you. You're good on the mat and good in school and and you're not a jerk about it. You let me down this week. You let yourself down. You let your family and your team and the school down."

I just listened and kept my mouth shut.

"You're a better man than this, Connor. Don't forget that."

"I'm sorry, Coach. I won't let it happen again." I seemed to be saying that a lot.

"I know," Coach said. "Now go finish your lunch. Word is, you have work to do. I expect you to be the first on the mat come Monday."

Mr. Orwal escorted me back in the middle of the passing period between lunches. In her own way, Principal Graff was a genius. She was so good at subtle cruelty; it was like she wasn't really human. That was another point in her favor as a candidate for carrying a *yokai*. As we walked, I tried to gauge Mr. Orwal, but he just looked bored like everything he saw was something he'd seen a hundred times before.

Who knew? If he were the *yokai*, maybe he had.

Susan was at her locker when I passed it. She gave me a look so angry it was like…well, like something that's really, really angry. I just sighed. I'd gotten numb about the whole thing. Maybe she'd calm down enough for us to talk. Maybe she wouldn't, and I'd be on my own again. Maybe I should take a vow of chastity and become a monk. I'd go someplace with trees and running water, and maybe find a panda to teach me the ways of kung fu.

Mr. Orwal led me out the doors and back to the loading dock.

CHAPTER FORTY-ONE

I stacked the last bag around 2:00 in the afternoon, a little more than an hour before school let out. I was policing the loading dock, picking up scraps of trash and sweeping away loose fertilizer, when Mr. Keranovak came up the path from the cafeteria. He surveyed the empty dock.

"Well done, young man. I don't think five kids in the whole school could have done it in a day."

"Thanks," I smiled at the janitor. "It wasn't easy, but I needed the workout."

"I bet you did." He looked at the dock again and whistled. "Morgan, for most of the kids here, five working together couldn't have done what you did. Like I said, you're a tough kid. Step into my office."

I followed him back the way he came. He led me through the halls and down some stairs to an area beneath the cafeteria. The small office had walls covered with paperwork on clipboards, an assortment of toolkits arranged on a long worktable against one wall, and a small desk that was empty except for a phone, monitor and computer. It was very different from Principal Graff's ostentatious room in the front office.

He sat down in a battered, leather desk chair and kicked a stool across the floor. "Take a break, kid. You've earned it."

"Thanks." The compliment felt good. I knew I deserved the trouble and lectures I'd been getting all day, but it was nice to hear something positive from somebody.

"Can I ask you a question?"

"Shoot," I said.

"It's kind of personal."

"No problem, Mr. Keranovak." Just about everybody had been getting personal with me all day. One more wouldn't make a difference.

"What's up with you this week?"

"I honestly have no idea."

"No, really. Something getting to you? I hear your dad's not really around. Anything you want to talk about between just us men?"

"Mom thinks it's hormones. She might even be right."

He looked at me for a long moment, then shrugged and slouched deeper into his chair. "Fair enough. I can't figure out why I did half the stuff I did when I was your age."

"Weren't you in Bosnia when you were my age?"

"Herzegovina, but I won't hold that against you. I won't tell you any war stories, either. Not today, at least.

On the other hand, here." He'd been digging around in a cooler under the desk. His hand came out with a six-pack of beer. He pulled one free and then tilted the pack toward me. "Close the door, tough guy."

"Holy crap, Mr. Keranovak," I said.

He mistook my surprise for a thank you. "No problem, kid. You worked like a man today. You deserve to drink like a man."

"You could get fired just for offering. I don't want to get you in trouble."

"I'd only get fired if someone reported me. He looked around the tiny office with his eyes held comically wide. "I don't see anybody in here who would do that."

"I wouldn't. Won't. But no thanks."

"I never heard of a man who won't take a free beer."

"I appreciate the offer, Mr. Keranovak. Really. It's just —"

"Hey, Connor, I get it. You're still torn up about the trouble you're already in. I can see how you wouldn't want to risk any more just now."

"That's not it. Well, that's not all of it. My dad, he's an addict. Booze, meth. I don't know what all else. Nothing against you, sir. You've been really kind, but that's just not my scene."

He grunted. "He's incorruptible, too. Your loss, kid. More for me."

"I know," I said. "Thanks again, anyway."

"No problem. You get on out of here. If you won't drink with me, at least you can get a half hour extra time off."

"Really?"

"Sure, kid. You did a day and a half of work already."

"Thanks. See you tomorrow?"

"Probably. Now get out of here and let an old man drink in peace."

I closed the door behind me and headed for my bike. As I rounded the corner, I saw a figure leaning against the wall. I tensed, thinking it might be DuPree looking for some payback, but the shadow was too small for that. As I got closer, it pushed off from the wall and stepped into the light.

It was Tasha, Susan's friend. School wasn't out yet, but normal school hours didn't seem to apply to her, anyway. Hadn't she rescued me at close to midnight because she was just hanging around?

"Hey, stud," she said. She used the same voice she always did when talking to me. Half-mocking, half-flirting. I never had figured out just what she meant by it. I was too tired to try and learn.

"Uh, hi." She worried me a little. In movies, the girlfriend's BFF was always the one doing crazy stuff to the ex-boyfriend. Like stalkers, it was only funny on a screen. I didn't want to experience it in real life.

"So," she said. "Like Oh Emm Gee. Ess Arr Ess Ell Why?" She stood in my way so I couldn't pass without pushing her aside.

I wanted to do just that, but instead said, "You could make a long list of stuff from this week that would work for. Most of them are my fault. Could you narrow it down for me?"

"Wow, big guy. Getting dumped makes you fierce. Why should I make this easy for you?"

"Because I'm too tired to do anything else hard today."

"I doubt that."

"Whatever. Tasha, I'm not in the mood. I haven't talked to Susan since the fight. I don't think she wants to talk to me. What did I do to you?"

"You didn't do anything to me, sport. Except maybe cost me a few hours of my life that I had to spend listening to my best friend cry. That wasn't on my agenda for the week."

"I can't give your week back. If I could, there's other stuff I'd fix first."

"Susan's mad at you. She's hurt and she's mad and she thinks she doesn't want to talk to you ever again."

"I know." The thought stole what little energy I had left. I wanted to sit down, lean against the wall, and take a nap. Whatever would happen with Susan would happen in its own time. I needed some real rest before I took it on. Besides, it wasn't going to happen on the sidewalk by the school in a conversation between me and her best friend.

"But, stud — and here's the thing — she was as happy as I've ever seen her when she was with you."

"Wait, what?"

"It was disgusting. Two weeks now of *Connor this* and *Morgan that* and long talks about your abs. Seriously, I wanted to hang myself with a jock strap."

I tried to think of something smart to say, but I had nothing.

"Well, shoot, stud. What are we going to do about this? I don't care too much about you, but I like it when my friend is happy."

"I like her happy, too," I said.

Tasha punched me in the chest. "Then do something about it, jerk."

"What should I do? What, exactly, do you want?"

"Dummy. She's waiting for you to apologize."

"She can't meet me halfway?"

"She could. But she shouldn't have to." Tasha punched me again, softer this time, then walked off in the direction from which I'd come.

CHAPTER FORTY-TWO

I came home and showered first thing, not that it did me much good. The manure smell of the fertilizer seemed to have gotten into my soul. I staggered out, ready for bed. The *oni* had left me, but I was still emotionally and physically exhausted. I wondered how I could possibly keep the demons out of me when I was tired to the center of my bones.

There was a knock at the door. If it was Susan, I didn't know what I would do. I didn't have the energy to give her what she needed or even to figure out what that was. I peeked through the peephole and saw Fiel's dark face and bright smile. He tapped the eyepiece with a fingertip, making me jump back. I opened the door.

He pointed at the towel around my waist, the only thing I had on. "What is it with you and being naked in front of people?"

I groaned. "You heard about that?"

"Bro, everybody's heard about that. They heard about it in Brazil. There's a dubstep remix on the YouTubes."

"What?"

"It's possible I made that last one up, but that's not important right now. What's important is that you come with me. Galhardo's in the car."

"I don't know." I was theoretically grounded. Mom had told me to consider myself on house arrest until she and I had time to discuss the full consequences of the past few days.

"Don't worry about it. My mom's cleared it with your mom. They think it will be good for you to be with people. The Xbox is fired up and we're not taking no for an answer. Just get dressed first, for crying out loud. I have little sisters."

Galhardo gave me a fist-bump across the back of his seat as I strapped in. He drove us into a neighborhood I couldn't believe belonged in the same school zone as mine. The houses were old and huge with lawns that had trees taller than you'd expect to see in the city. He pulled into a six-car driveway in front of a house almost the size of my whole building.

"Holy moly," I said. "Guys, are you rich or something?"

"Our dad is," Galhardo said. "He's an investment banker. Has Pee Aitch Dees in math and economics."

"He has to be," Fiel said. "Did I mention we have five brothers and four sisters?"

Their mom greeted me at the door as soon as it swung open. I'd never met her, but she grabbed me into a hug while shouting welcomes I didn't understand. She backed up, looked at my face then hugged me again hard enough to hurt. Mrs. Fortes was a small woman, no taller than my chest and trim like a model, but she was ridiculously strong. She would have done well on a wrestling team. She patted my cheeks with both hands at once, said something else I didn't understand, then bustled down a wide entry hall into some other part of the house.

"Wow," I said. "What did she say? I don't speak Spanish."

"Wouldn't help if you did," said Fiel. "That was Portuguese."

"You mean like from Portugal?"

"I mean like from Brazil. Mom and Dad are both from Rio de Janeiro." Fiel grabbed my collar and dragged me through a door, down some stairs and around a corner.

He'd said the Xbox was set up, but that wasn't the whole story. They had four machines running on four flat-screen TVs, all running connected with a four-way split-screen shoot-em-up game. It was a LAN party running full swing in a basement full of soft furniture, comfort food and loud kids.

"I thought you said there were 11 kids in your family?" At least 20 people were hanging around in the basement.

"No," Galhardo said. "My parents have 11 kids. Six of them have kids of their own. Fiel and I are younger than some of our nephews." He ducked through the crowd, distributing hugs, noogies and arm punches all around.

We played for a few hours, and I got my rear end handed to me whenever I took a turn. I'm quick, but I never get any practice with video games. Even Sol, the youngest nephew in the room, schooled me whenever I saw his character on the screen. That was okay, though. Love and a spirit of family filled the room. It fed me, filling the holes the *oni* had eaten out of my spirit over the past week. I was in a home, surrounded by people who loved each other. Because of Fiel and Galhardo, they loved me, too.

Mom and I had that kind of connection, but because of moving around and who my father was, that was all the family I had. This was something new to me, and I liked it a lot.

I don't know how Mrs. Fortes knew, but it was exactly what I needed.

I stayed until around 10:00. Fiel and Galhardo drove me home. When they stopped in my lot, I said, "Um, guys?"

They looked over their shoulders, mirror images staring over the center of the front seat. I started to sweat, wanted to chicken out, but I was tired of keeping secrets from people I knew I should trust. Besides, if Fiel and Galhardo couldn't handle it, who could?

"Um, you know how I had some weird stuff go on early this week?"

'Yeah," Galhardo said. "Do you want to talk about it?"

"Talk as much as you want," said Fiel. "Can I request a slow-motion replay of you serving DuPree a can of grade-A, premium whoop-ass? That guy's a total jerk."

"It's more than that," I said.

Galhardo said, "Man, you look so nervous. What's the deal?"

"Um," I started. I shut up again. These people were

just beginning to accept me, and the evening with their family had felt so good. What if my weakness got me kicked out? I'd be alone again. I wasn't sure I could handle that.

"Come on, man," Galhardo said. "There's nothing you can't tell us."

"Unless you're coming out of the closet," Fiel said. "There's nothing wrong with that, far as I'm concerned. Just don't start saying about how you're into me."

"You?" Galhardo said.

"Why not me?"

"Come on, really?"

"Thing is, guys," I said. "I didn't hit DuPree."

"Heck you say," Fiel exclaimed. "I saw you do it."

"It wasn't me. An *oni* did it while it was inside my head." I looked at them both, shifting my eyes to each of their faces in turn. My stomach felt sour.

Fiel laughed and not a short chuckle. It was a long roll of belly laughs all the way to his toes. He looked like he was having a seizure. Galhardo held himself together better, but he was laughing, too.

"Oh, man," Fiel said between gasps, "That's all? That's what you've been worried about? Brother, demonic possession's an occupational hazard for us. We thought you were depressed or something, having some kind of breakdown."

Galhardo said, "It happened to me last summer."

"Too right it did," Fiel said. "You came back from that date with what's her name, and you were all *none of your business* this and *f-bomb* that. You scared little Sol to death and Mom yelled at you until you cried."

"I didn't cry," Galhardo said.

"Yes he did," Fiel said to me. "When the *oni* popped out of him — Mom's kind of scary — I killed it while her back was turned."

"I was a shadow of myself that day," Galhardo said.

Fiel stared at him for a moment. His mouth moved silently. Finally, he said, "I got nothing."

Galhardo said, "Man, none of us is perfect. We take risks. We tussle with demons. Sometimes we take a hit. That's how it is."

Fiel asked, "Have you talked with Sensei about it?"

"No," I admitted.

"We did. Do you know what he said?"

"What?"

"He said, 'I know.' Told us wounds are part of being a warrior. Sometimes they get inside you. The trick is learning how to make it less likely and to recognize what it feels like.

"So he won't be mad?"

"He won't even be surprised," Fiel said. "Look at it this way. Would it have been possible to adequately describe what it feels like to be possessed by an *oni*?"

I thought about that. "No," I said. "No way."

"No," Galhardo said.

"Right. So now you know what it feels like and you'll know if it happens again."

"Thanks," I said. After a moment, I nodded. "Really, thanks."

I went upstairs and collapsed onto my bed. I was even more physically wrecked than before my friends had come to get me. But my mind felt fresher and my spirit was beginning to heal. If I took the effort to *look,* I believed I would see a bright spark of hopeful light at the center of my *dan tien*. Exhausted as I was, I sat up to wait for Mom. She'd been great that morning and I wanted to say thank you. Besides, it wasn't like I needed to be alert in the morning. It would just be more of the same.

CHAPTER FORTY-THREE

Turns out it was more of exactly the same. When I got to school, Mr. Orwal escorted me straight to the horticulture buildings. He didn't even let me go inside first. Mr. Torres was waiting for me, scratching his head and holding a bright-yellow sticky note in his other hand.

When he saw me, he shrugged an apologetic look in my direction. He exhaled with a kind of raspberry sound and pointed to the bags I'd stacked neatly the day before. "Wrong place. Mr. Keranovak says we make a mistake. They go in the supply shed."

"Okay," I said. "Which supply shed?"

He pointed toward a corrugated plastic structure near the cafeteria.

"That one? The one right over there?"

"Si."

"You mean the supply shed next to the loading dock?"

"Si."

"The supply shed that's 10 feet away from where the bags were when I started?"

"*Si.*" He slapped me on the shoulder a few times then went off to do his own job.

I didn't even have it in me to grumble. Today would be a waste of my time no matter what I had to do. Stinking like manure for the second day in a row wouldn't be my favorite part, but a confused and often frightened teenager in the middle of a supernatural war's gotta do what a confused and often frightened teenager in the middle of a supernatural war's gotta do.

Meaningless manual labor can hypnotize you quickly, which I guess is why it's always part of the training montage in old kung fu movies. By the time I moved my fourth bag, I'd slipped into a rhythm. I focused on my body mechanics, on empowering my movements by expanding the growing ball of power in my *dan tien*. When I got it right, which wasn't often but happened more and more as the day went on, the bags felt about as heavy as my school bag.

I kept my feelings positive and the power in my center calm and relaxed to guard against resentment or frustration that could let an *oni* back into my mind. I thought about Mom and Coach and about how they kicked my butt while still letting me know they cared. I thought about Sage's fierce friendship, Alex's kindness and the cheerful support of Galhardo and Fiel. People cared about me, and I cared about them. It wasn't a family with a mommy and a daddy and Spot the dog in a two-story house with a picket fence and last year's SUV in the garage. But it was a family, and I hadn't had that before besides Mom.

Maybe she was right about my dad's time in jail.

Maybe we could stay put long enough for me to really become a part of the Bushido Champions.

Maybe.

Even Susan wasn't an entirely lost cause, at least not according to Tasha. *One crisis at a time,* I told myself. *Save the world first then think about how I'm going to get the girl.*

I ate lunch alone under a tree by the shed and then got back to work. I didn't see much sense in spending the whole hour of lunch sitting around. When the closing bell rang, there were still a dozen or so bags remaining. I stretched myself, my back popping as I bent backward with my hands on my hips. When I straightened out, Mr. Keranovak was walking toward me.

I waved. "Hey, Mr. Keranovak."

"Hey yourself, Mr. Incorruptible. How'd you do today?"

"Almost finished. I must have been more tired than I thought."

"No problem. You killed it yesterday. I'll have one of my guys finish up next week." He turned back toward the cafeteria building.

"Mr. Keranovak?"

"Yeah, kid?"

"Would it be okay if I finished tonight?" It was the right call. I'd feel better if I finished, and even at my slower rate I'd be done well before wrestling practice let out. Mom was working late and Susan wasn't talking to me. I wouldn't miss anything.

He looked pleased, but not surprised. "Sure thing, kid. I thought you might say that. It's part of your incorruptible character. Knock yourself out. Just check in with me before you go home."

I got to it. The last bags took less than an hour, but by the time I finished the sky was nearly dark. Winter in Portland does that. I stretched my back again and looked at the stacked bags. I couldn't even smell the fertilizer anymore.

Movement across the field grabbed my attention — a flash of shadow over the gloomy green lawn. I scanned the grass between my position and the school and saw nothing in the dark. I unfocused my eyes, letting my peripheral vision scan for movement, and then I saw them: six *oni* sliding toward me through the twilight. I could hear their legs swish through the grass of the field.

I wasn't *looking*, but I could see them moving the grass as they came. They'd manifested physically, like the others had last week in the woods. That meant just one thing: they were coming for a fight.

CHAPTER FORTY-FOUR

My bike was locked up next to the bus ramp on the other side of the school. Reaching it would mean running through a campus full of *oni* fat and happy on the misery of my classmates. No escape that way. Even at the edge of the grounds, away from the main flock, they had me outnumbered six to one. *Oni* were weak individually, but if one snuck into my head while I was fighting others … I wasn't eager to repeat that experience.

The demons closed in, faster now that they knew I'd spotted them. They skittered like bugs, darker shadows racing across the dark of the school lawn. I looked to the horticulture buildings. They were a short sprint away, but there was no way out the other side. I could use the close quarters to fight the demons one at a time, but if they overran me I'd be trapped. That left the cafeteria building.

My legs moved before my brain even finished the thought. Wrestlers aren't the best distance runners ever, but we can sprint like we mean it. Blame that on what happens during conditioning to the guy who comes in last. I rounded the nearest corner of the cafeteria building yards ahead of the *oni*. Their howls filled my brain without making a sound. The crunch and slither of their pursuit was right behind me.

I sprinted full out for the next corner and sped past the loading dock at top speed. Shadowy claws clicked on the pavement behind me. The *oni* had already reached the side of the building. Only one turn left before running would just drop me back into the field. At the next corner were the school dumpsters, which were surrounded by a short wall with the chain link gate still wide open. If I were quick enough, I could get inside one and close the lid before the *oni* got to that side of the building.

I didn't hesitate. I sort of wished I had.

I popped the lid up with one hand, high enough to get in but not so high that it would stay open, and vaulted over the edge. The lid was already closing as I slid through the gap and it slapped my head with a heavy plastic thump just as my feet hit the bags of garbage. The dumpster was half full, so I had to lie down in the stinking mess. It reeked of sour milk, rancid ketchup and French fries gone bad.

I've mentioned how gross school food is, but I never thought about how bad rotten school food might be. You learn something new every day, I guess.

Claws clattered on the pavement outside. The demons came in from two directions and stopped next to my dumpster. If I'd run straight ahead, they would have caught me for sure. Hissing and growling came from what I imagined was a football huddle of *oni* trying to figure out where I'd just gone.

They were using strategy, trying to pincer me between two groups. The *yokai* had to be behind the attack, making another move against me specifically. Between the fear from that realization and the stink of the school garbage, my stomach rolled and pitched. I felt the puke coming just in time to turn my head and open my mouth wide. It flowed out of my body as quietly as I could make it happen. Then the vomit smell hit me and I puked up some more. I was just glad for the darkness. Another look at my lunch would have triggered a third go.

After my stomach settled down, I listened carefully. I waited, counting slowly to 100. On the way, I had to puke two more times, but they were light and mostly liquid by then. It wasn't hard to keep them quiet.

At 100, I poked the lid of the dumpster up with one finger, just enough to peek one eye over the edge. I saw no big gang of *oni,* but one stood watch about 10 yards away. It was thick and birdlike, more like an eagle than the crane that had ridden DuPree that night. It perched on the edge of the loading ramp, swiveling its head in all directions. If I left the dumpster, it would see me.

I put the lid back and thought, turning my face down in case I needed to barf again. I was getting used to the smell, but if I was at the wrong angle and it made me cough, the *oni* would hear me. The lookout would see if I ran for it and bring the rest of the swarm in moments. I could try to wait them out, but *oni* don't sleep. They'd be on the prowl until daylight, which was more than 12 hours away. Even if they never thought to search the dumpster, I didn't think I could handle spending the whole night in that dark, tight, stinking place.

Trash settled beneath me, and something poked into my hip. I shifted my weight, figuring it was an old food can or one of those tiny cartons of milk. The something moved with me. It was in my pocket, just my cell phone.

My cell phone.

Quietly, very slowly, I snaked my arm down to my pocket. Every time I made the trash rustle, I stopped and counted to 50 before moving again. After what felt like 300 years, I had my phone in my hand and up by my face. I scrolled through my contacts until I found someone who could help and understand, hit "Call" and covered the speaker with my thumb. I could hear if I strained and would just have to hope the person on the other end could hear me.

Sage picked up after four rings. Kind of.

"You've reached Sage Kaiser. I'm not available at this precise moment. Please leave a message at the tone and I'll do my best to get back to you right away. Thank you."

Alex was next on my list.

"Connor. Thank God," Alex said. Her voice was loud and shrill even through my thumb. "They're coming. They're at the doors." She screamed and dropped her phone. In the background, I heard claws clicking across a wooden floor.

Alex was under attack, too. What was going on? Was the *yokai* moving on all of us, all at once? Suddenly,

Sage's call going to voice mail felt like very bad news. A fist of fear squeezed my guts and I gagged again. Nothing came out.

Ironically, it's harder to stay quiet when you're dry heaving than when you're actually puking something up. I must have managed it, because nothing came to throw open the dumpster and put me out of my misery. When I had myself under control, I called Fiel. He answered on the second ring.

"Connor, you too?" I started to talk, but he cut me off. "Can't talk. Call Galhardo. Do it now." He sounded stressed, and I heard tires squealing. I hit "End" and scrolled to the number. Galhardo answered immediately.

"On a scale of one to 10, how bad are you right now?" His voice was very calm. Traffic sounds echoed in the background: brakes, tires and a blaring horn. Fiel was swearing.

"I don't know," I whispered. "I'm hiding. They haven't found me, but I can't move without giving away my position."

"Call that a four, four-point-five. Where are you?"

"School. Dumpster by the cafeteria. Next to the loading dock."

"You're between us and Alex. She's a nine, but we'll grab you first. You can help us help her. Don't say 'okay.' Just be ready. We'll be there in … six minutes. We'll honk. You'll run." He hung up.

I looked at my phone, glowing in the dark of the dumpster. Everybody was under attack, and they'd come after Alex in her home. I thought of Mom. What if they'd sent *oni* to attack my apartment? I scrolled through my list and found her number, then thought better of it. No way could I explain this in a way that made sense, not in time to be of any help. I scrolled some more and called Mrs. Dochevnya.

"Hello?"

"Mrs. D.," I whispered, "this is Connor."

"Strange boy, why are you whispering?"

"I'm hiding. The *oni* — the shadows — are after me."

"Where are you? I can come?"

"No, Mrs. D. I'll be all right. Other people are coming to help me. But they've attacked some people at their homes. Can you check on Mom?"

I could hear Mrs. Dochevnya's wrinkled smile all the way through the phone. "Always the good boy. Of course I will visit your mother. But not to worry. Is rare for shadows to attack openly one who does not know them for what they are."

"Are you sure, Mrs. D.?"

"Am I sure? Are you sure you know how to play your wrestling game? Yes, strange boy, I am sure. And if I am wrong, they will regret it. For a little while."

"Thanks, Mrs. D."

"Go now, good, strange boy. I will see to your mother."

Something heavy landed on the lid of the dumpster. I almost dropped my phone into the trash, but caught it with my other hand before it could slide into the muck. I hit "End." Claws scrabbled on the slick, sloped surface inches from my head as whatever was up there struggled to stay on top. Probably not a squirrel.

I heard sniffing, again with my mind instead of my ears. The *oni* on the lid was searching for me, like it had heard me talking but didn't understand how dumpster doors worked. I held my breath and tensed my muscles to spring. If it figured out the lid, maybe I could pull it in and tear it apart before the other *oni* saw.

The claws scraped some more and slid down the lid all the way to the edge. I heard a thump on the pavement below. I wanted to laugh, but that would just be another hint for the *oni*. The claws clacked away on the pavement.

I breathed again then jumped and hit my head as a car horn sounded three long blasts right outside. I threw the lid up, jumped out, landed wrong and rolled into a stand after leaving a patch of skin and denim on the sidewalk. A four-door sedan was sideways along the dumpster, headlights blazing. Fiel sat behind the wheel and the rear door nearest me stood open. Sage waited in the back seat, sitting all the way across.

Again came the howls of the *oni*, hissing through my mind like sandpaper. Shadows moved on the rooflines and in the bushes. I sprinted and dove headfirst into the car, landing with my face in Sage's lap. The car moved before I could close the door. The turns and speed bumps threw me around as I struggled to sit upright and fasten my seat belt. I pulled the door shut as we sped out of the parking lot and onto the street.

"Are you injured?" Galhardo asked from the shotgun seat. His voice had the tone most people use to ask, "Would you like fries with that?" He was looking at his phone. To Fiel, he said "Turn left at the main road."

"No," I said, "just scraped."

"And filthy," Sage said. "Seriously, Morgan. You could have hidden in a rose garden or something. You stink like the lunch lady's breath."

"Turn right at the next light," Galhardo said.

"Sorry," I said. I rolled down my window.

And the *oni* poured in.

Two leaped past me before I could even react. I pushed on a third one with my left hand as I groped blindly for the window crank with my right. The demon squirmed around me into the car, but I caught a fourth with the window itself. I rolled the handle with both hands until the monster split open like a cracked egg, vanishing in a dark mist. I could see others clinging to the outside of the car, but no more got in.

We had enough trouble as it was. Something was down in the footwell clawing at my shins. Another *oni* had climbed onto the back of Fiel's seat and was yanking on his seatbelt. The car swerved across the road as it choked him with the strap. Claws scraped across the roof as demons slid off to splat on the pavement behind us.

Galhardo said, "Turn right in two blocks. There will be a yield sign, but not a stop sign." He didn't look up from his phone. Behind him, Sage grabbed an *oni* with both hands and started head-butting it with savage precision.

I grabbed the *oni* on Fiel and pinned it to the back of the driver's seat. It writhed and slashed at me with dark claws. With my free hand, I pulled a pen out of my breast pocket. I thumbed off the cap and stabbed the demon six, seven, eight times before it collapsed into reeking smoke.

Sage's *oni* was also gone, leaving just the one trying to eat my shins. Sage undid her seatbelt and leaned over to grab it. She lifted it into the air and I stabbed it until it, too, dissipated into oily shadow.

Slowly, carefully, I felt in the foot well for the cap of my pen. I found it, put it in place, and put the pen back in my pocket. Sage fastened her seatbelt. We looked at each other in wide-eyed silence.

Galhardo said, "Turn left here. It's the fourth house on the right. We've seen it before."

Fiel said, "Who opens a window in the middle of a fight? Can somebody tell me that?"

"This guy," Sage said. She drawled "guy" out so it lasted five or six syllables. I couldn't help but laugh. Galhardo laughed with me, then Sage, then Fiel. It was nervous laughter, the kind you get after you've been scared. But it was real and it carried the positive feelings that drive *oni* away when they're only in spirit form.

It lasted until Fiel stopped in front of Alex's house. All the windows were dark and the lawn was shrouded in shadow. A figure lay face down in the middle of the grass, its blonde hair so pale it seemed to glow against the background.

Alex.

CHAPTER FORTY-FIVE

Sage pulled a flashlight out of her pocket and shined it through her window at Alex. We could see blood on her back and hair even from inside the car. She was moving, but weakly.

"It's a trap," Sage said. "Where's the second bomb?"

"The second what?" asked Fiel.

"The second bomb. My dad was a Marine medic in Iraq and Bosnia. He says terrorists usually set two bombs. The first would hurt a bunch of people. The second was set for later to take out the rescue workers."

"That's … evil," said Galhardo.

"Yeah," Sage agreed.

We peered into the night, into the darkness. I scanned the roofs, the shadows in Alex's doorway and the line of trees along the driveway. No sign of *oni*, but that didn't mean they weren't there.

"Anything? Anybody?" Fiel asked.

"No," I said.

"No," Sage said.

"Nothing," Galhardo said.

"Ambush," said Sage. "Even if there's nothing, we plan for it to be there. I know first aid. I can find out if it's safe to move her. Connor, you're with me. We should be strong enough to carry her. Galhardo, I need you out but hanging back. You'll watch for trouble and keep the path clear. Fiel, stay tight and be ready to move. Questions?"

"No," said Fiel, then me, then Galhardo.

"Okay. On three. Connor, come through my side of the car. We'll leave the door open." She counted down and exploded out into the night. I threw myself out right behind her. We ran to where Alex lay. Sage took a knee and placed her hands on either side of our friend's head.

"Hush, Alex," she said. "It's us." She whispered, asking questions about pain and how her neck felt. I tried to look everywhere all at once. The wind blew, pushing branches around. It was hard to tell what movement was important and what was just normal.

Sage said to me, "I think she's okay to move. She's cut and still bleeding, but her spine and neck are okay. Okay enough to risk it. You get her chest. I'll grab the legs."

I moved to stand by Alex's head. Sage and I rolled her over. Alex took in a sharp breath, but she didn't scream.

Galhardo did.

"Connor!" he yelled. I dropped to my knees and covered Alex's head with my body before he could say, "Watch out!" Something dark whooshed through the air where my face had just been. Sage soccer-punted it into the night.

"More coming," Galhardo's voice was still calm, raised just enough to be heard. Something crunched against the side of the car. I hoped it was an *oni*.

I slid my arms through Alex's armpits as Sage hugged her legs. We ran for the car. I couldn't see much from my position, but I felt Galhardo moving ahead of us. His sword whooshed as he cleared a path through the monsters that were swarming now.

Sage steered me by turning Alex's legs like the rudder of a boat. I ran backward, half my speed coming from Sage's forward motion. My legs hit something hard and I sat down in the back seat then scrambled backward to pull Alex in with me. Sage followed and slammed the door.

I looked around, checked every corner. Galhardo was already inside with us and no bad guys had followed. Fiel floored the accelerator and we were moving again. Through the rear window, I counted more than 20 *oni* scrambling after us.

Sage turned on the dome light to see Alex more clearly. Our friend's shirt and one leg of her pants were soaked through with blood. Her breath was quiet, thin and ragged. I *looked* at her for a moment. Her *dan tian* still glowed with life force, but it was weak and gray.

Sage leaned forward and tore open Alex's shirt. A jagged gash ran from her collarbone across her chest and toward her belly button. Blood still ran through what was left of her bra.

"Knife!" Sage shouted. Galhardo handed a multitool over the top of his seat without taking his eyes off his phone. He said to his brother, "Right on Couch, three blocks ahead."

Sage cut free a big patch of Alex's shirt. She wadded it into a ball and held it out to me. I took it in one hand, confused. Sage pushed Alex's bra up to her neck and pressed my hands down on one slashed breast. "Do you know first aid?"

"No," I said. I was confused and embarrassed. Alex felt warm and sticky through the wadded-up fabric.

"Press down as hard as you can." She must have seen the look on my face because she smacked me lightly on the cheek. "Don't worry about that right now. You're saving her life."

Galhardo's voice sounded far away. "Take a right here. Run the sign. *Run* it. Sensei will know what to do, but he needs time to do it."

I pressed down with the cloth, hoping the experience wouldn't ruin breasts for me for the rest of my life. I thought of Susan. If we got back together, this would be high on the list of things I never, ever told her about.

In the other seat, Sage tore open what was left of Alex's pants. She found the other cut and pressed down on it with her bare hands. I focused hard on my part of the job.

A horn blared outside and Fiel braked so hard I almost lost pressure on Alex's wound. He made a sharp turn and accelerated. Galhardo said, "That was special. Four more blocks, then left. Move over one lane."

I heard another sound then, a sharp double-whoop. Red and blue lights cut through the air around us.

Because of my dad, I knew what that meant. Fiel slowed the car and pulled over.

The police officer approached our car. I looked over my shoulder to see him walk toward us, flashlight high in his left hand. He shined it through the windows. When the beam hit Alex, he froze. His right hand went to his gun.

"Connor," Sage whispered, "roll down your window."

Keeping one hand pressed hard against Alex, I did.

The officer pulled his gun out. He held it down along his leg, but he kept it ready. I could tell from his wide eyes that he was starting to freak out. It's not every day a cop sees a half-naked, bloody teenaged girl in the back seat of a car.

"Officer," Sage said. Her voice was loud. Not like she was yelling, just clear and with a tone of command.

The officer shuffled closer to the car, but not so close that I could reach him through the window. "I need you all to put your hands on top of your heads," he said, using the same clear, commanding tone as Sage.

"Officer," Sage said. In front, Galhardo and Fiel put their hands on their heads. They laced their fingers together on top. I started to move, but Sage shook her head.

"In the back. Hands on your heads. Now!"

"Officer," Sage began again.

"Both of you. Move slowly. Hands on your heads."

"Officer —"

He shifted his gun to point it into the back seat. "Now."

"Officer," Sage repeated. She continued in a rush before he could interrupt, "we are both applying direct pressure to this girl's wounds. If we move our hands, it could kill her. She's hurt. She's our friend."

The officer seemed to relax, but he didn't lower the gun. "Suppose you tell me what happened. Stay calm, now."

"We were supposed to pick her up and go out tonight. When we got to her house, she was like this in the front yard. We're taking her to the hospital. Can you escort us?"

He lowered the pistol, but didn't holster it. With his free hand, he grabbed a radio mounted on his shoulder. "I need an ambulance at the corner of Couch and 22nd."

A voice came over the speaker. "Couch and 22nd, van en route."

He put the radio down and holstered his weapon. "How about I bring the hospital to you? In the front, please step out of the car and sit here on the ground."

CHAPTER FORTY-SIX

The five of us sat on the wrestling mat at the dojo, licking our wounds. It was Sunday afternoon. Dealing with the police and the hospital had taken the rest of Friday night. Dealing with our parents had taken all of Saturday. Mom wasn't thrilled about my going to train after what we all told the police was a gang attack, but I explained how I wanted to check on my friend's recovery and even that didn't work until I suggested I would be safer there than at home alone.

Most of us wore bandages. Alex's wrapped over more than 20 stitches the ER surgeon had put in her. The space smelled of salves and ointments from the front room. Sensei sat with us. None of us were in shape to practice, but we still took the time to be together. We'd gotten our rear ends kicked in the surprise attack, but we were all alive. Alive and angry.

Alive and angry and ready to be the next ones to make a first strike.

Sage said, "Does anybody still doubt that we need to move now?"

Nobody said anything.

"Does anybody doubt it's Principal Graff?"

We didn't have much more clear evidence than we had the week before, but I explained about her shadows during my meeting on Thursday. Fiel and Sage nodded as I spoke. Mr. Orwal was still a possibility, but Graff was definitely the front runner from what we could tell.

Alex said, "I still have some doubts, but at this point acting and being wrong will be worse than waiting until we're sure."

We were all quiet. Outside, the sounds of rain and traffic somehow made the silence that much more intense. After a while, I said, "Okay. Do we have anything remotely resembling a plan?"

"Ride 'til we find them," Galhardo said. "Kill them all."

"What?" I said.

"Huh?" said Sage.

"*The Thirteenth Warrior?* Antonio Banderas? Remake of *Beowulf?* Nobody?"

We all just stared at him.

"I swear, people, it's like you think movies were invented this century."

I said, "A friend of mine on the debate team says Principal Graff usually leaves right after sports practices finish. She's not the last to leave the building, but she's usually alone in the parking lot at that time of night."

"Who do you know on the debate team?" Sage demanded.

"Don't ask."

"I just did."

I ignored her. "Graff always parks in her reserved spot at the corner by the cafeteria building."

"Three paths come together there," Alex said. "One from the front doors, one around the corner from the cafeteria, and that short one in the courtyard. If we come at her from all three at once, she won't be able to see us all until we're on top of her."

"Are we really talking about this?" Fiel asked.

"Are you really asking?" Sage said. "What have we been talking about all afternoon?"

"I know, but I mean, we're talking about ambushing our own principal."

"No, we're not," I said. "We're talking about freeing our principal from possession by an elder demon."

Fiel nodded. That was the hard truth of it, no matter how much we wanted to pretend it was something else. He said, "So we catch her where those paths converge."

"Right," said Sage. "Galhardo, Alex and Fiel can wait in the library until practice is over. Connor and I will take the front doors. Alex, take the courtyard. You two can take the cafeteria path. We'll meet in the middle."

"When?" asked Alex.

"Will you be all right by tomorrow? Soon beats late here."

"I won't be 100 percent, but I can be there. I won't be any better by Tuesday or Wednesday."

We broke apart soon after that, each of us going our own way, quiet in our thoughts. Sensei bowed us out and watched us go. His face was as blank and impassive as ever.

My phone buzzed when I was halfway home. I looked down at the text message.

SUSAN: Can you talk today?

ME: Not today. I want to talk with you, but I'm in the middle of something important.

SUSAN: I'm important.

ME: I know. You're important. You're important to me. Tomorrow? Please?

SUSAN: OK.

ME: Wait! Busy tomorrow, too. Tuesday? Promise?

SUSAN: I don't know if I can wait.

ME: Try? I know I don't deserve it.

SUSAN: OK. I'll try.

ME: Thanks.

She didn't sign off with an X or an O, but at least we'd had a conversation. Maybe we could patch things together, assuming I was still alive on Tuesday to keep my promise.

CHAPTER FORTY-SEVEN

I paced in my room. Five steps from my open door to the wall by the window and five steps back. Mom was at work again, and I was nervous. My stomach rolled like in the moments before the first match of a tournament.

"Am I really going to do this?"

Did you say you would? said Coach Gable.

"Yes, but …"

But what?

"But this is more than training with a bunch of people and seeing scary shadows on the walls. This could destroy my life. I mean, forget suspension. Forget being expelled. I could end up in jail." I didn't even mention the harm we might do to Principal Graff, harm she wouldn't deserve if we were wrong.

Kyle said, Are we agreed this is real?

Two out of three, said Cael.

"Three out of four, counting me," I said.

Not the best odds, Cael said.

But they're the odds we've got, said Kyle. Not much choice but to play them.

Break it down, said Coach. What's the worst that could happen if you do this?

"We beat up a principal and she's normal. She presses charges. We all go to jail."

That is pretty bad, Kyle said.

What I'm saying, Cael said.

And the worst if you don't? Coach asked.

"Demons take over the school. They hurt my friends. People die. News spreads and feeds *oni* all over the country. Maybe the world."

We're agreed that's worse, right? said Kyle.

"Yes," I said.

Yes, I think so, said Coach.

Damn it, Cael said. Yes. That is much worse.

Yes, Maynard finished the vote.

"So I do this," I said. I rubbed my face with my hands and sat on the bed. My legs felt weak.

And really do it, Cael said.

I thought you disapproved, Kyle said.

I do, but if you go in halfway you'll get yourself and everybody on your side hurt. Maybe dead, said Cael.

Go 100 percent, Coach said. Even if you get hurt and only have 60 percent of yourself to give, give all of what you have left.

"All right," I nodded. "Okay." If this were a movie, we'd have all put our hands in a circle and said something manly. But this wasn't a movie and they were just posters who gave good advice.

Sleep came surprisingly easy after that. I'd made my decision and wouldn't change my mind. Once I'd done that, it wasn't really different from being ready for a match. There wasn't a lot of sense worrying about what I couldn't change. If we lost tomorrow, I'd be with my friends, helping them fight the good fight. My only regret would be that Mom would never know why I died.

CHAPTER FORTY-EIGHT

It was time. I sat on a bench in the locker room feeling the sweat from practice dry on my hands and face. I figured if I got in the shower, I'd find a way to keep washing until it was too late to move. Besides, there was a fair chance I'd get dirty again before the night's work was through.

I breathed as deeply as my tense stomach would allow. I felt tight, wound up and disconnected from my *dan tien*. That would probably fade once things started. It usually did.

I don't pray. Mom never took me to church and my dad was never around to talk to about that kind of thing. But I did close my eyes for a moment. I thought of Mom and my grandmother and my dad's parents. I whispered to myself and to anybody who might be listening, "If I can't make it through this, at least let me make them proud." I stood up and walked out of there.

Sage was on the other side of the doors. Neither of us said anything. We just fell into step and walked the long way out, down the main hall to the front door. I'd never noticed before, but Sage could keep up with me stride for stride. Not a lot of people, and almost no girls, were tall enough to do that.

We sat by the bus ramp on concrete slabs that served as benches. They felt cold through my jeans. Sage and I sat front-to-front, looking over one another's shoulders so we could see the whole area. I watched the parking lot. Sage kept her eyes on the door. We were alone in the night, just us and a few teachers' cars a few yards away. The others would be around the corners, just out of sight. It never occurred to me to wonder if they would be there.

As we sat, our breath came out in clouds like we'd started smoking. As if. We wouldn't have to wait long. From what we'd seen, Principal Graff was usually out the door no more than 10 minutes after practices ended. She probably had some kind of rule that made her stay that late, and she left as soon as she was allowed.

My phone vibrated in my coat pocket. Amped as I was, I nearly jumped out of my clothes. I fumbled it out with shaking fingers to find a text message from Mom.

MOM: Your girlfriend is here.

ME: ???

MOM: Susan is in the apartment. Sitting on the couch.

ME: What is she doing there?

MOM: Crying. Please 2 advise.

ME: IDK

MOM: What's an IDK?

ME: I Don't Know

MOM: Did I mention the waterworks?

ME: Yes. IDK Mom. I have to stay after practice

MOM: How long?

ME: IDK. Please 2 advise

MOM: Hurry home. ICWICD.

ME: ???

MOM: I'll C What I Can Do

ME: You're the best

MOM: I know. Get done and get home.

ME: OK

I blew out a long breath in a puffy, white cloud. Was this karma? If so, which kind? Was the universe rewarding me by sending Susan to my house to make up? Or was it punishing me by sending a crying Susan to bond with my mother while I went toe-to-toe with a demon?

Sage said, "What?"

"Susan stuff."

"You two are still a thing?"

"Don't ask me. I don't know."

"No time, anyway," said Sage. A door closed behind me and I heard the click of Principal Graff's heels. They got louder as she closed the distance with a brisk, steady pace then stopped as she came up beside us.

"Mr. Morgan," she said. "Miss Kaiser. What are you two doing here so late?"

Sage said, "It's not late for us. Practice just let out."

"Did it? I hadn't noticed."

"Yeah. Coach kicked our a—" Sage started, "worked us hard tonight. I'm surprised I'm not steaming out in this cold."

"Are you waiting for a ride?"

"Yes, ma'am."

"Both of you?"

"Yes, ma'am."

"But, Mr. Morgan, I was under the impression you rode your bicycle home. Coach Russel tells me it's rather your trademark."

I choked. We hadn't planned for this. Sage came to my rescue, "That's right, ma'am. He's waiting for my ride. He didn't want me to have to wait out here alone in the dark."

"How chivalrous," Principal Graff's voice was thick with innuendo.

"We could see you to your car," I said. I winced. It had come out too fast, too eager. I could almost see her thoughts shifting from judgmental to suspicious.

"Noooo," she said, drawing the word out. "I wouldn't want to trouble you."

"It's no trouble, ma'am."

"I insist. You two sit right where you are. Don't miss your ride on my account." She studied us for a long moment, then turned and walked toward her car. The boxy Volvo was maybe 50 paces away.

We sat, eyes wide, staring at each other. Principal Graff's shoes clicked away on the pavement. I counted 20 paces then we stood up to follow. Ahead, she had stopped. I could see the shadows of Galhardo, Fiel and Alex around her in an arc. They were blocking her path. She was talking by the time we caught up and closed the circle.

"Other schools may tolerate this kind of gang intimidation, but I assure you we here at Ponderosa

High do not. I will be in contact with Mr. Orwal and the city police first thing ..." she trailed off as she noticed us behind her.

Her eyes widened. She seemed afraid, like any woman alone would be when surrounded by five hostile people. But behind that fear, I saw anger. Anger and maybe hunger. The security lights on the walls nearby dimmed from yellow to orange.

"Hey, lizard face." Galhardo drawled. "Look at me when I'm insulting you."

"It's only polite," Fiel cooed.

Principal Graff's head snapped back to them. "Young man, how dare you speak to me in that tone? How dare you call me names?"

"Aren't you the one who's always telling us good citizens are truthful?" Sage said from behind.

"Yeah," said Fiel. "You gave me three days of hard labor for lying about a homework assignment. Aren't you happy we've learned that valuable life lesson?"

"Do you want more of the same, young man?" Principal Graff glared at Fiel. Behind her, Sage clapped her hands together. Graff spun to face Sage, one hand clutching at her own chest.

"She moves fast for a crazy old bat," Sage said.

"Crazy, stupid, ugly old bat," Fiel said.

"Crazy, stupid, ugly, mean, arrogant, silly old bat," Galhardo said.

"Don't forget incontinent," I said.

"Incontinent?" Sage whispered to me.

"I thought we were making things up," I whispered back. Principal Graff had turned to face Galhardo.

The back of her neck was red with rage.

But she didn't break. As the insults mounted, she grew very still. She didn't even seem to be breathing. In the gap between one rude word and the next, she shouted "Children! You are behaving like little boys and girls. Like naughty grammar-school students. I will discuss this with your parents, and the police, in the morning. Now, I must insist that you let me pass. Get out of my —"

Alex cut in. Her voice lacked the sing-song taunting tone of Galhardo and Fiel's insults. It was cold and flat like somebody reporting bad news on television. "Out of your nasty little school? I'd love to. Have you seen the test scores? The state and district reports? Only the most incompetent, possibly delusional principal in the state could be responsible for Ponderosa's performance metrics and come to work with her head held high."

Principal Graff froze. She swiveled her head toward Alex. Her eye went bright and cold. "What did you just say to me?"

"This is the second year that your school failed to meet performance standards," Alex kept up the attack. She'd done her homework and knew how to hit where it hurt. "What kind of principal lets that stand?"

Our principal's voice got smaller, a weak vibration in the night. "Please, children. If you have a complaint, have your parents call me ..."

"I know what mine call you," Galhardo said.

"Incompetent," said Alex. "Sub-par. Below average."

"Not yet meeting expectations," I quoted from my 4th-grade report card.

"I will certainly call each one of your parents."

"As if mine would interrupt their day for a call from someone as insignificant as you," Sage hissed.

"Then school security. The police," Principal Graff pleaded.

"Pray they're better at their jobs than you are at yours," Fiel said.

Principal Graff reached into her jacket and pulled out a black smart phone. Alex's hand shot out and snatched it. She moved gently without touching the principal, but so fast I could hardly tell her arm had moved.

"Miss Magnusson," she gasped. "That is highly—"

"Stow it, you old sweat sock," Galhardo sneered.

"You can have it back, Principal Graff," said Alex, "when you bring our school test scores, staff compliance and lunch program up to regulation standards."

"By which she means, never," said Sage.

"Just like," Alex said. She was whispering now, the truth behind her insults loud enough to carry them forward. "Just like you'll never get out of your half-assed, middle-management, nowhere, dead-end, public-school job. You soulless, talentless, hopeless, helpless, hapless, ineffectual bureaucrat."

"That … that is ENOUGH!" Principal Graff screamed. There was a vibration beneath her voice, something rough and powerful and dangerous. She started to shake, her whole body at once, like she was freezing or having a seizure. She fell to the ground, smacking her head on the pavement with a loud clap.

Wow, I thought, *we've just killed our Principal. I wonder what jail will be like.*

She lay on the cold pavement, breathing shallowly but steadily. Black, oily shadows leaked out of her eyes, ears and nose. They rose knee-high, then hip-high, then tall as Galhardo as they formed the shapes of 12 shadow monsters with the bodies of lions with scorpion tails. They stood around her in a tighter version of the circle we had formed. They were bigger than the other *oni*, looked stronger and better fed. Worse, they didn't look like a *yokai* at all.

The demons leapt to the attack. One swept both claws at me in a hug. I clinched its neck and rolled it to the side. That didn't seem to hurt it, but it did whip the thing's stinging tail away from my face. I swept my head around to see how the others were doing. Galhardo had cut one monster in half with his sword and was fighting to parry the stings of two more. Sage divided her attention between a pair of the things, hitting each just enough times to stun it before turning to the other. Fiel ducked and weaved through the mob, distracting *oni* who missed him by inches with fangs, claws and tails. Alex had fallen back. An *oni* separated from the scrum and charged her. She lashed out with a toe to kick it in the throat. As it fell, she pointed above and behind me and shouted, "Look!"

I spun around and kneed my *oni* in the chest three, four, five times then drove its face into my knee. Its head exploded and I was alone. I looked where Alex was pointing. Not all of the *oni* from the school were coming our way, but there were enough that I couldn't see the ground beneath the swarm. We were outnumbered, vastly outnumbered, with enemies inside and outside our circle.

And there was no *yokai* in sight. We were outnumbered, and we were wrong. I saw Principal Graff, unconscious on the sidewalk. My mind flashed to my psychology project, to Enigma — a program of disinformation to trick an enemy into showing his hand. She'd been a trap all along.

CHAPTER FORTY-NINE

Sage shouted, "Form around Alex!"

I didn't hesitate. Sage had been right too many times before. I crouched to get my weight low and charged for where I'd last seen Alex. Lion shadows with vicious stinging tails moved in from all sides, but they were light, made from shadow, and I knew how to tackle. I charged through them almost like they weren't there. I didn't take any of them out of the fight, but they didn't stand a chance of stopping me.

I got to Alex's side with just a mouse over one eye. It was already swelling, but I couldn't say exactly how I got it. Sage was already there, standing with her hands flexed into claws. She was roaring — literally roaring like a tiger. Her eyes blazed. Galhardo and Fiel were still among the *oni,* moving together like two parts of the same body. They destroyed two of the monsters on their way toward us. Both times, one brother made the kill when an *oni* exposed itself moving for an apparent weakness in the other.

Again, I thought of Principal Graff and Enigma. Had the *yokai* done that to us? Led us to attack a false weakness so it could drop the hammer once we exposed ourselves?

The smaller *oni* were closing fast. As the brothers reached us, Sage started shuffling backward toward the courtyard nearby. We followed in a pack keeping our eyes toward the enemy. I understood her plan. The courtyard was narrow, with a plastic roof to keep out the rain. On the other side of that opening, we could keep the *oni* from swarming us. We'd be outnumbered, but not outflanked. It might give us a chance.

I looked at my friends. A line of cuts ran down one of Sage's shoulders. The brothers weren't hurt, but their breath came in sharp gasps. Alex had a streak of blood on her leg where she must have torn out some stitches. We were all worn out and every last one of us was confused by what had happened. We'd been so sure.

Sage's plan might not give us a good chance, but it was still a better chance than we'd have surrounded in the open.

Sage grunted, not with pain but with effort. I noticed for the first time that she was dragging Principal Graff by the collar of her suit jacket. I shuffled closer and took a grip on one shoulder. For a little old lady beset with demons, she was surprisingly heavy. The courtyard had closer, brighter lighting than the parking lot. It felt like stepping into daylight as we backed up the final few feet.

Only six of the large *oni* had survived our initial battle. They were hanging back where we'd fought. Wave after wave of smaller *oni* swarmed around them.

"Just like in *300*," said Galhardo, staring out at the massing crowd of demons. There were dozens, maybe hundreds, massing for the attack.

"What?" asked Alex.

"*300*. The movie. Gerard Butler. Battle of Thermopylae."

"I got nothing," Alex said.

"Seriously, people. Movies have been around for more than a hundred years. You should try one some time."

Sage said, "Wait. I saw that one. Didn't they all die?"

"Hey!" I shouted. "Spoiler!"

The little *oni* gathered around their larger cousins, forming a ragged line at the edge of the parking lot. They weren't smart, but they were cunning. They were clever enough to think about what chances they had against a group that had killed a half-dozen monsters twice their size. If they mobbed us, they'd almost certainly win, but it wouldn't go well for the *oni* at the head of the line.

"You happy now, Alex?" Sage growled.

"Not really," Alex leapt onto the bench of a picnic table. From a higher position, she would have better reach and angle on the small demons.

"You hate to say you told us so," Fiel said.

"I love to say I told you so, but tonight I'll make an exception."

Galhardo stood straight, pointed his sword at the line of demons. A yellow gleam reflected from the security lights along the blade. He shouted, "Yo! Slim Shady. Come get some."

"What just happened?" I asked. I took a position

next to Sage, guarding Principal Graff's still unconscious form.

"We were wrong," Sage said. "It wasn't her."

"What do we do?" Fiel asked.

"You mean right now or later on?" I asked.

Sage snorted. "Optimist much, Morgan?"

The *oni* growled, almost as one creature. They didn't move, but I felt a vibration in my *dan tian* that said they were building momentum. My heart pounded in my chest and my legs felt weak. I looked everywhere, searching the courtyard for help, escape, anything. There were no windows and the heavy steel doors would be locked at this hour. We were alone.

"What a stupid place to die," Sage muttered. She let go of Principal Graff and drew herself into a fighting stance.

"Then let's not do that," I said. I don't think the others heard her. Their focus was farther away.

Sage rolled her eyes at me. The whites were unusually big. The growls of the *oni* rose in pitch, the noise ripping through our psyches despite the eerily silent courtyard. Sage still stood over our principal in a protective posture. The old woman was unconscious, but breathing in a steady rhythm.

"Here they come," said Alex. I didn't look up. My body wouldn't let me. I couldn't stop staring at Principal Graff.

"Will they care how many of them we take with us, do you think?" asked Fiel. I heard his feet slapping on the pavement in the rhythmic dance step of capoeira, a move called a *ginga*.

"I will," said Galhardo.

"*Chuugi,*" Alex shouted, "you with us?"

"Yeah," I answered, still staring at Principal Graff.

"Imminent peril here, buddy," said a voice. I think it was Fiel's, but that wasn't important. There was something else, something urgent about the unconscious woman in front of me.

"Five seconds, I figure," said another voice.

"Been a pleasure, people," said Galhardo.

Something about Principal Graff. An idea was nibbling at my brain, but I couldn't grab hold of it.

Out in the rest of the world, one voice said, "*Gi.*" It wasn't a scream, but it was somehow louder than the sound it made. It carried that power I'd felt in class, and it rang through my *dan tian* like a mallet hitting a bell.

Half of my mind dope-smacked the other half. I had more important things to think about than Principal Graff. But no, part of me insisted, I didn't.

Two voices called out, "*Yuuki.*" At the edge of my vision, Galhardo thrust his sword forward, daring the first demon to impale itself on the tip.

She was the principal of our school. The big cheese. She should have been the *yokai.* It was the perfect position for maximum trouble, with power and access like nobody else. She couldn't *not* be the one. But she wasn't.

Three voices said "*Jin.*" I felt the power of the words carrying the spirit of the people who'd had our names before us, even as I focused on our principal.

Power and access. She had power and access.

Four voices said *"Rei."* From what seemed a long way off, the *oni's* claws scrabbled on the concrete. They were almost on us.

Access. She should have been the *yokai*. She had access to the whole school.

My friends said *"Makoto,"* all together. It was almost like they were singing.

Access! Principal Graff had access! She had keys, the master keys to every door in the school. That included the ones behind us.

"Meiyo."

I dove at her unconscious body and tore through the pockets. There was nothing in them. She didn't carry a purse, either. She must have dropped them. The *oni* were just yards away. I patted her down one last time, almost missed the shiny glint on her index finger. She'd had the ring looped around it. I slipped them loose and shouted, "We are leaving!"

I leapt to my feet and ran for the doors. Sage saw immediately what I was up to and followed, dragging Principal Graff behind her. Alex, Galhardo and Fiel moved more slowly, keeping a fierce eye on the approaching shadows. They were an incoming wave, a tsunami of darkness and hate.

I ran through the keys. Car. House. A big one with the words DO NOT DUPLICATE printed on both sides. That would be it. I slammed it home and turned it. Something inside the lock clicked. Sage's hand shot forward and yanked the handle. The door opened like this kind of thing happened every day.

"Go!" Sage shouted. "Go! Go! Go!"

I grabbed Principal Graff through the armpits and dragged her through the door. Alex left her position and ran through at a full sprint, leaping over both Graff and my bent-over body. Galhardo and Fiel wove past, and Sage darted in behind them. She pulled the panic bar with both hands and slammed it shut. Claws screeched on the steel of the opposite side almost immediately.

Nothing moved in the wide common area of the school. I focused my chi and *looked* in every corner. The halls were dark, lit only by safety lights set into the walls at eye level. A few *oni* roosted here and there, on top of lockers or under tables, but they didn't even seem to see us. Whatever was giving the monsters orders outside wasn't talking to these.

Fiel leaned his back on the thick concrete wall. His knees sagged and he slid to the floor.

"*Chuugi,*" he whispered, "good thinking."

"Yes," Alex panted. She held both hands tight against one thigh. Blood seeped into her jeans in a widening red blot.

Galhardo said, "You know that part in all the horror movies where the victim can't make the keys work? Or drops them? Or whatever?"

"Yeah?"

"I'm so glad that didn't happen."

Fiel was the first to laugh, but not by much. Sage slapped my chest with a backhand, and Alex hugged me tightly. The brothers flashed me a high five from where they sat by the door, hugging each other and laughing like they were crying.

I laughed, too. It wasn't that funny, but you don't get to cheat death every day.

At that moment, Principal Graff opened her eyes.

She wasn't laughing.

CHAPTER FIFTY

Principal Graff's eyes blinked, then focused. They darted to each of our faces. Nobody moved. It was as quiet as, well, I can't think of anything else that quiet. It was like we were all afraid that breathing would make her angry.

I was closest to her. Her eyes fastened on mine. She looked confused and maybe a little frightened, but she didn't look angry.

"What … what's happening?" Her voice sounded as scared and confused as her face looked.

"Principal Graff," I said. I kept my voice as calm as I could, which wasn't very calm.

"Mr. Morgan, why am I lying on the ground in the school's common area?"

"Principal Graff," said Fiel. We walked into her field of vision so she could see him. "Please don't move. You've had a head injury and we're afraid you've hurt your neck."

I stared at him. Behind me, Alex gasped. Galhardo stood quickly and walked past the top of our Principal's head, where she couldn't see him. The look on his face told me why.

"Hurt my neck?" she said. "How? Was I unconscious?"

"Yes," Fiel said. His face was honest and serious, shining with concern. "We were meeting Sage and Connor after practice and we found you here. Do you remember slipping? Were you climbing up on something? Making some kind of repair?"

"I don't remember doing that. I don't remember … much."

I got it, then. *Oni* possession left people's memories fractured. If Fiel did this right, we could get out of it without being expelled, put in jail, then grounded for a year after we got out. Of course, we still had to find the *yokai* and somehow survive dealing with it. But this was right now. That was later.

"Just rest, ma'am," Alex said. She shuffled up and knelt beside the woman. She kept her voice low, soft and even. "We'd give you a pillow, but I don't think we should move your head."

"Have you called an ambulance?"

"We were about to, then you woke up," Alex said. She kept her voice gentle.

"Do you know where the school phone is? The room-to-room phone by the door?"

"Yes, ma'am," said Sage. She crossed over and picked it up. It was an old-style phone that was attached to a wall unit with a curly cord. You couldn't call outside with it, but you could reach different rooms inside the building.

"Please call extension 413. That's Mr. Keranovak's office. He should be in at this hour. He'll know what to do."

Sage picked up the phone, dialed and waited. Alex covered Principal Graff's right eye with an open palm, then lifted it. She did the same for the left eye. I'd had that done to me often enough to know she was checking for brain injury.

"I'm pretty certain you have a concussion, ma'am," Alex said. "I'm afraid I don't know how to test for a neck fracture without risking worse damage."

"Thank you, Miss Magnusson."

Sage hung up the phone. "No answer."

"I know where his office is," I said. "Galhardo, let's go get him. He'll be around someplace."

I trotted down the halls, Galhardo right behind me. The empty dark made the school eerier than normal. We slipped down a flight of stairs to the maintenance areas under the cafeteria. Ahead, dim light shone from Mr. Keranovak's open office door. It wasn't the bright light of overheads, just the flickering light of a computer monitor.

The office looked like it had a couple of days earlier. The walls were still covered with clipboards and forms. Well-organized tool kits were still arranged on the work table. The monitor, computer and phone were the only things on the desk. Mr. Keranovak's foot protruded from under his chair.

I almost missed it at first, but there was his work boot and the cuff of his coverall uniform. He lay on the ground, unconscious, almost completely under his desk. His chest rose and fell is slow, deep breaths.

"Do you smell booze?" I asked.

Galhardo shook his head.

"Then he was possessed, too."

"We'd have seen something by now. I mean, he's Mister Keranovak. He's everywhere."

"Any other ideas? Go get Alex. She knows this stuff."

He ran down the hall, his uneven footsteps echoing creepily.

I reached for the phone. We could get into real trouble for this, but Principal Graff, and maybe Mr. Keranovak, would need actual medical help. More than Sage or even Alex could give. Besides, they would both want to talk with adults about stuff like this.

My hand stopped over the phone in front of the monitor. There was something about it, about the image on the screen. I looked closer and recognized my apartment building in a browser window. It was a satellite image from Google maps next to directions from the school. A window beside it showed my student record in dim, green letters, including my name, Mom's name and our address.

Power and access, the *yokai* needed. The ability to go anywhere without being questioned. A principal wasn't the only person in a school who could do that. A janitor had that, too, even more sometimes because in a school people always notice the person in charge. I'd never seen any *oni* on Mr. Keranovak, either. I'd just assumed it was because he was happy, but what if he carried the *yokai*? He lay by my feet now, abandoned by a spirit that had most likely manifested to physical form. A demon capable of harming humans directly, of tearing them apart with claws and fangs. A demon who knew where Mom and Susan were.

I ran.

CHAPTER FIFTY-ONE

I ran faster than I had ever run before. Faster than that night with DuPree and his pals. Faster than when the demons had chased me around the cafeteria. I sped past my friends and out the front door before Galhardo had finished telling them about Mr. Keranovak's office. I burst through out into the night and pounded across the pavement. At least I had my shoes on this time.

Oni fluttered down from above, clawing at my head and face. I went through them without even slowing down. After the first few slammed limp on the ground, the others kept away.

The bike rack was ahead, mine the only bicycle left on it. I kicked the thin rail without breaking my stride. It didn't budge, but I didn't have time to fumble with the lock. I breathed in and focused all the fear, all the confusion, all the pain from the last few hours until my *dan tian* glowed with it, then I pushed all of that energy through my hip and down my leg with a second kick. The rail broke off with a sharp crack. I ripped my chain off the loose end and pumped like my life depended on it. Like my mom's life depended on it. Like Susan's life depended on it.

My record getting home was just over five minutes. I hoped it would be fast enough. I sped through the night — my helmet left behind in my locker — past tall trees and up the long hill past the community center. It was only a few minutes, but it had never felt so long before. I had so much time to think, so much time to imagine what I might find. I'd seen Mom hurt before, too many times. I'd seen Susan covered with blood. My blood, but the image left nothing to the imagination. The *yokai* had already been alone with them for who knew how much time. It could be torturing them, could have already killed them.

I could find my apartment door standing wide open, with two mangled corpses the only thing to welcome me home. The image seemed so real, the glowing center of my chi started to boil like it had the day the *oni* had possessed me. I tried to turn that energy back to the clean power I'd felt before. I couldn't let the dark ideas take control, couldn't give the *yokai* any edge it might use to peel away my strength.

A car I'd missed while I was thinking about what might happen pulled out right in front of me. I braked hard and swerved, slammed a foot to the pavement to keep upright. The driver laid on his horn as I sped past him. I pushed my legs even harder to make up for the lost seconds.

When I turned the corner a block from home, I could see Mrs. Dochevnya's door open, light spilling through it onto the wet pavement. Mrs. D. could help them; maybe she was already helping them. I crossed the street, jumped the curb and leapt from my bike, legs never breaking stride. I ran up the steps in two long leaps. Behind and below me, my bicycle crashed into the side of a dumpster. I was full of power, hot with it. I'd never felt so strong in my life. If something were threatening my mother or Susan or even Mrs. Dochevnya, that something would not live to see the sunrise.

I bounced off the wall at the top of the stairs and skidded along the walkway. I grabbed the doorknob. It was unlocked and I almost fell as I burst through the door.

The first thing I saw was Mrs. Dochevnya lying on the floor. She was limp and motionless, but I didn't see any blood. I couldn't tell if she was breathing or not.

The second thing I saw was Mom and Susan sitting on the couch. They were staring forward like they were watching TV, but neither was facing the screen. Their eyes were blank and their hands lay still by their sides. Neither moved except to pant shallow breaths. Mom's white scrubs looked pink to me through the haze of red that filled my vision at the sight of them like that.

The third thing I saw was the *yokai*. It looked vaguely human, or at least human-shaped. It was tall, pudgy and entirely white. Not the bright white of a summer cloud or a good light bulb, but a sickly, dirty white. The white of toadstools and pus. Its face was featureless, but mouths covered its whole body. More than a hundred sets of white, gummy lips opened and closed with wet, sucking sounds. Some were screaming. Others cried.

Some cursed me in languages I didn't know and maybe nobody had known for a thousand years. My stomach lurched and rolled at the sound of it.

Above that obscene chorus, the *yokai*'s voice was a deep, powerful bass. "*Chuugi*," it said in an echo of Sensei's greeting what felt like years earlier, "I've been waiting for you."

CHAPTER FIFTY-TWO

I howled and lunged toward the thing, murder in every atom of every cell of every part of my body. The *yokai* shot out claws from the tips of all its fingers, holding the talons just inches from Mom's and Susan's throats. Neither of them moved or even seemed to notice the danger. I froze in mid-leap.

The roaring furnace of energy at my center turned cold and grey as ash. Where there had been power and anger there was only fear. If Mom or Susan got hurt here, it would be my fault. I would have failed them both, utterly. Nothing was worth that.

"Ah, ah, ah," the demon said. I glared at it from just a foot too far away. I was much bigger than the thing, but it had those claws. I might be able to kill it, or save Mom, or save Susan, but never all three. Probably not even two. We were all helpless before the *yokai*'s power.

"What do you want?" I tried to sound calm, but my voice shook with fear.

"Oh, the usual. Confusion. Suffering. Pain. Power. But for you, *Chuugi,* I want so much more." Its mouths cooed and ahhed as if agreeing with the monster's main voice.

I said nothing. The *yokai* went on. "You couldn't tell? I complimented you, flattered you, even offered you alcohol. Really, Connor Morgan, I should be insulted."

It was right. Mr. Keranovak had been giving me special treatment since the day I came to Ponderosa. If I'd put it all together earlier, maybe I could have attacked the *yokai* on my terms with my people at my back. But I was too stupid, too blind, too weak, and now I was in this position and my family would pay the price. I looked past the monster and saw my posters through my open door behind it. Maybe some magic could bring them to the rescue, bring them to life to help me destroy this thing and save the people I cared about. But no, they just hung there on the wall.

I was alone, abandoned. Even my power, my chi, seemed to have left me when I needed it the most.

"Ahhhh. Now you understand, little boy. That's all right. You humans can be depressingly slow of thought. Never mind, I still have an offer for you."

I kept quiet.

"You sign on with me. Betray the rest of that rabble when they arrive to help you. It won't be too terribly long if they follow the same breadcrumbs I left for you. Once they're dead, you help us with what the master has in store for you all. In return, you live. Your mother lives. This girl lives, and as a bonus she loves you just the way you've always wanted her to."

The mouths all over its body puckered up and made kissing noises at me. Pale white tongues protruded lewdly and licked at rotten skin.

"It's who you are, after all. Look how easily you hurt your girl and that Neanderthal at the school, how quickly you embraced the anger and despair that are part of your place in life. How easily you lied to your mother and your friends. You belong with us, Connor Morgan. It's where you've belonged all your life."

The monster was right. My whole life had been a string of terrifying events, violent upturns and abandonment just when I got attached to anybody or anything. This sense of belonging I'd felt in the past few weeks was an illusion. How could anybody care about someone as weak and pitiful as me? Why should anybody in the whole world deserve a life better than mine? The cold pit in my *dan tian* sparked with a red anger at the easy lives some people — including most of my "friends" in the Bushido Champions — lived compared to mine.

"Ahhh, there is anger there," the *yokai* crooned. "I can give you power, little one. What you felt as you leapt up the stairs to face me? Nothing compared to what I can teach you to control. You will be mighty. Mighty enough to punish everybody who hurt you and to keep anything that would threaten you or your mother quivering with fear."

The mouths twisted into a perfect, terrified grimace. A hundred voices begged me to spare them, pleaded for my mercy. The red coal in my center grew and filled me with a terrified, furious strength. I stood straighter and felt my own mouth twist into something someone else might have called a smile.

"Very good, very good. Do we have an agreement, then?" The voice of the *yokai* massaged my mind, calmed me and excited me at the same time.

It was a simple choice. Save my family by betraying the Bushido Champions or watch Mom and Susan die. It was a no-brainer, really. On one hand, power and acceptance for who I am. On the other, my family dies because I stay loyal to people who love who they want me to be. The *yokai* was right. It knew where I came from, who I really was.

I looked at Mom. She would understand. After all, hadn't she betrayed my dad when it came to choosing between him and me?

As if it could read my mind, the *Yokai* smiled. It smiled with all of its mouths, everywhere on its body. The word *yes* whispered across my mind, sparking little explosions of anger at things people had done to me over the years. *Yes*.

CHAPTER FIFTY-THREE

Yes. The word felt as good on my mind as a sports massage on tired muscles. It would mean the end of fear, the end of helplessness for me and Mom and even Susan. *Yes*.

But behind the word there was something else. Not a word or a thought, just the face of Coach Fagin and behind it Coach Gable, Cael and Kyle, and Mom and Mrs. D. All of the people who loved and cared about me. Behind them came Sensei and Fiel and Galhardo, Sage and Alex, all the people who made up my family. They might not have been flesh and blood kin, but they were family. They knew me, knew my faults and failures. They wanted me to be better than I am, but they loved and respected who I was. The *yokai* couldn't offer me that; it could only offer to take it away.

"I'll pass, thank you." My voice carried all the strength of the red-hot anger that had been filling me, pulsed with the hate the demon had fed me and that I was throwing back directly at it.

The *yokai* turned its flat, featureless face directly toward mine. I felt the intensity of its gaze even though it had no eyes. "Are you certain?"

Behind the creature, I saw my posters again. The men I hoped to be like some day. Behind them I saw the faces of the Bushido Champions, and not just the friends I'd trained with for the past weeks. I saw a line of faces I'd never seen but somehow knew, traced backward maybe all the way to the beginning. I knew they were the men and women who had carried my name and my responsibilities in the years and lives before I was born.

I nodded, keeping my eyes on the center of the demon's face. None of those people would make a different choice if it were one of them in my place.

"Then you have chosen to suffer," its voice sounded neither happy nor disappointed with my decision.

My power vanished; the spark of red rage was gone leaving just cold, terrified grayness in my *dan tian*. I nearly fell as the strength left my legs and back. My arms, which a moment before had been ready to grab for the *yokai,* fell useless to my sides.

"And suffer you will," the *yokai* said, "but not just you, little creature. This is so beyond you, beyond even me. Bigger than … but no. I shan't spoil the surprise."

"Go ahead and tell me," I spat. My mouth felt loose and foreign in my face. Even my tongue was exhausted. "I won't be around to see it."

"Oh, but you will. You will. I don't plan to kill you, stupid child." It cackled like something evil cackles when it thinks about hurting a living being. "What example would that set? A warrior's death is nothing to the warrior. Your Sage Kaiser covets such a death. No, no, nononono. I plan to break you. Your friends will see what you have become and their souls will lie open for my pets to feast upon."

It stroked Mom's cheek with the claws of one sickly white hand. A single tongue protruded from the palm and licked her neck. It whispered, "You know you can't save both of these scrumptious morsels. Even one as large and quick as you can't do that. But I'm fair in my way. I'll let you choose who lives. You simply have to betray the other, like you did tonight when you abandoned your friends."

My throat squeezed shut and I fell to one knee. I struggled to get my breathing back to normal, struggled to move with the furnace of my life force a heap of cold, barren ash. Pictures of Mom bloodied swapped back and forth through my mind with images of a broken Susan.

The *yokai* sniffed deeply as if enjoying the smell of a favorite meal. I could almost see the despair wafting off me and into its nonexistent nostrils. It would have closed its eyes if it had any.

"Delicious! Delicious, isn't it, mortal? You'd die right now. You're as ready for it as any of your silly little allies. But are you ready to watch others suffer for your decisions? To choose who suffers and screams and begs, asking you why you abandoned her?"

I looked everywhere for help. Mrs. Dochevnya lay on the floor. Mom was still motionless. No sirens or running footsteps sounded in the night beyond my still-open front door.

"And she will suffer, whomever you choose. This will not be quick."

I looked to my posters, but they offered no help. Just Kyle's determined eyes in a swatch of light from the window. *No Excuses,* he'd written. I still owned an autographed copy.

"And I will make you choose, little warrior of loyalty. In the end, you will choose."

I thought of what Kyle fought through to become a best-selling author and motivational speaker. I *felt* weak and drained, but I had all four of my limbs. No way was I weaker than he was on his worst day. In the ashes of my *dan tien,* a spark lit.

Short time, Morgan. Short time. I fed the spark with deep breaths, felt it ignite and glow not with the red anger the *yokai* and *oni* had created but with love and loyalty and hope.

"I will make you betray the —"

I hit the son of a bitch mid-monologue while its mushroom-pasty jaws were still flapping. I hit it low and hard with a vicious double-leg takedown that carried us both into the kitchen, away from the couch. The little mouths gasped and shouted and some sprouted fangs that bit my face and arms. I yanked its legs up and the thing fell hard, slamming its head on the edge of the stove in a clattering thud that shook the whole room.

It would not make me choose. It didn't own me. I owned me. This demon could kill me, could still kill us all, but it would do it on my terms. I am Connor Iraeia Morgan. I am *Chuugi.*

I.
Betray.
Nobody.

CHAPTER FIFTY-FOUR

Here's how it is about sucker-punching a *yokai* and slamming its head against the business end of a cheap apartment stove: It doesn't like it.

The demon didn't even pause as it grabbed me by the neck and threw me through the kitchen table. The table collapsed in a heap and our computer threw out sparks as it slammed into the floor. Papers and plates flew through the air. Our ketchup, salt and pepper rolled wildly across the living room floor.

"You insolent puppet!" the *yokai* shrieked. It stalked toward me, giving me its full and undivided attention. Its mouths were all closed into tight, disapproving frowns. At least it wasn't threatening Mom or Susan anymore. They were safe until the thing skinned me alive and ate my flesh like a fresh batch of human jerky. After that, it probably wouldn't stop with just me.

It stood on top of me before I could even sit up, stomping down with one pale foot. I rolled out of the way and it splintered the remains of our table instead. Something shattered and when the *yokai* lifted its foot, shards of dinner plate protruded from the sole. It didn't seem to notice. It stomped again with the same foot. I rolled the other way, avoiding the monster's foot by less than an inch. The sharp glass still embedded there grazed along my arm.

I gasped and scrambled, avoiding stomp after stomp. Every few seconds, Mom or Susan would pass through my confused line of vision. They still sat motionless as if all this were happening on a bad TV show. The demon screamed and threatened above me. As I rolled through the remains of the table, I saw our salt shaker lying on a pile of school papers. Mrs. Dochevnya had used salt to kill an *oni* after it had grown fat from feasting on my mind for days. Maybe it would work on the thing's master. I army-crawled to grab the tiny bottle just as the *yokai*'s foot came down on my ankle. Shards of plate went all the way through and the bone snapped with a sickening crunch. I screamed, but I held on to the salt. The mouths on the *yokai's* foot and leg extended their tongues to lap up my blood as it ran down the sides of the glass.

I reached up with my other hand to unscrew the cap. The *yokai* kicked me hard in the ribs with its other leg.. The shot knocked my hands open. I flew in one direction, the salt in another. I landed hard on the couch between Susan and Mom, my wind kicked completely out of me. I hurt, but the couch had cushioned the worst of the impact. Landing against the wall would have broken my back.

CHAPTER FIFTY-FOUR

The demon walked toward us slowly, savoring my fear and the white-hot pain in my ankle. "I am going to break your spine and leave you to watch me eat them inch by inch." Its many mouths smacked their lips together, slurping hungrily. They licked their lips, all the lips each tongue could reach.

I stared at the mouths, my ears ringing. My whole head was fuzzy and out of focus. Something was happening, but I couldn't piece together what it was. Reality had become a jigsaw puzzle, poured into my senses straight from the box.

Above me, the *yokai* spewed out words in an obscene torrent of angry syllables. I couldn't make sense of them. My gaze roamed randomly around the living room, landing from time to time on a single object. A photo on the wall. Mom sitting to my right. A broken dinner plate on what was left of a chair. The shaker of salt. Susan, paralyzed and helpless to my left.

The *yokai* hit me across the face. It wasn't a punch or a rake with its talons, just a contemptuous backhand like my father used to give me when I spilled his beer.

"Are you listening, mortal?"

My head rocked to the side and I saw Mom again. Mom, and Susan on the other side. The pieces fell together in a rush, all the fear and danger all at once. We would die if I didn't move, and if the *yokai* kept its word, we'd die worse than I could imagine.

I threw myself forward and past the *yokai* with all the strength I had in my good leg. It slashed at me with both hands, but I was too low. I rolled into the debris where the salt shaker had fallen.

"I'm going to start with their toes, human. You and I will savor their agony together, one bite at a time."

My hands ran through the pile, finding the salt shaker despite their trembling and the screaming distraction in my injured leg.

"I will feed you their eyelids and make you enjoy the taste."

I tried to unscrew the top, but my hands fumbled once, twice. The cap didn't budge.

"You will hear every scream as I break them like forgotten toys. You will watch every instant!"

I flexed my arms as hard as I could, pouring energy from my *dan tian* like Alex had when she bent my arm in practice. The shaker broke between by palms. Pieces of glass cut into my flesh. Salt stuck to my sweating hands, the grains like fire on my wounds.

"When I'm through with them, I will eat you over the course of days." It reached down to grab my wounded ankle, squeezing on the torn skin and broken bone. The mouths on its palm bit into me.

I screamed and grabbed its arm with both salt-covered hands. Its skin immediately started to smoke and bubble. It shrieked and dropped me, clawing at the smoking pits in its arm. The mouths there sprouted blisters and boils. They roared with a millennia worth of rage and pain, all in different pitches and voices. I rolled past the monster and scrambled into the kitchen where I grabbed the counter and hauled myself onto my good leg.

I flung open the cabinet doors as the demon howled behind me. It had already stopped screaming and was turning its agony into a rage it would use to tear me apart. I felt its presence, its intent, its desire to hurt me wash over me like the blast wave of an explosion.

Never before had I wished so hard that Mom was more organized. I threw cabinet contents over my shoulder, bouncing them off the *yokai* as if they could do any real harm.

Captain Crunch. Olive oil. Three empty cocoa cans.

The *yokai* leapt over the wreckage in the living room, landing three steps from where I leaned against the counter's edge.

Mac and cheese. A box of raisins. Half a bottle of Bailey's Irish Cream.

It flared its arms wide, claws out, preparing to slice me into bite-sized pieces.

Top Ramen. Pop Tarts.

And there it was: a blue container with a picture of a girl in a raincoat. I grabbed it and spun, my leg almost collapsing under my weight. I opened the spout and swung my weapon in a wide arc. Red, ropy lines smoked across the *yokai's* chest, arms and face. All of its mouths shut tight in a desperate attempt to escape the burning. I shoulder-butted the monster to the ground and sat across its chest, the pain in my ruined ankle forgotten. I poured the rest of the salt onto its head, where its face would have been. I dropped the empty box so I could rub the stuff into the demon's pasty flesh with both of my hands.

The creature thrashed beneath me, but already it was losing strength as whole pieces of its neck and face sloughed off and dissolved into stinking smoke.

It wailed and cursed and battered feebly at my chest and arms. Its mouths no longer wailed. I pinned it and watched it burn — until a sword flashed across its throat and the entire body disappeared in a grease of vapor.

I fell forward and rolled to my back. Galhardo and Sage looked down at me. My eyes closed.

CHAPTER FIFTY-FIVE

Considering what happened in the hours just before I lost consciousness after a life-and-soul struggle with an elder demon, what happened next was boring. I wasn't there for most of it, since I woke up in the hospital later that night. Sage says Mrs. Dochevnya woke up soon after I passed out and took charge.

Alex took Susan home. She wouldn't remember anything and the situation would be complex enough without getting her involved. Sage left with Fiel and Galhardo once Mrs. D. explained that she knew enough to take care of everything. She told the police I'd fought off a home invasion robber after he knocked out Mom. They believed her and called an ambulance for me. I got some Demerol, an Aircast boot and the news that I was done for the rest of the wrestling season. My leg would heal all right, but not in time for regionals that year.

It was a small price to pay, considering. Besides, I wouldn't be the only athlete to work for a scholarship after an injury. It just meant training that much harder once I recovered.

Mom dropped me at school Tuesday morning. She wanted me to stay at home, but let me go when I reminded her how much class I'd missed the week before on in-school suspension. I got out of the car using a hard, hickory cane Mrs. D. let me use instead of a crutch.

When I turned to wave goodbye, somebody attacked me from behind. I spun out and away, feeling a light punch on my spine and a sharp pain in my ankle. Fiel stood there next to Galhardo. I could tell they were both exhausted from last night's action, but they also looked proud and pleased to have scared me into the next week.

I sighed. They smiled even wider. Galhardo jerked his head at our school. "Look at it. *Look* at it."

I *looked*. A few *oni* crouched on the roof, looking lonely. It was nothing like I'd come to expect. The air around the school seemed brighter. Looking at our classmates as they shuffled through the front doors, I thought I saw more smiles than before.

"Feels good, huh, *Chuugi*?" said Fiel.

"Yeah," I said. "Yeah, it does. We saved the day. Nobody knows it was us, and we can never tell, but we sure saved the heck out of it."

"Like Bruce Wayne or Peter Parker," Galhardo said.

"Say," Alex said, "I think I've heard of those guys." She had come up behind the brothers and wrapped them up in both arms. She moved carefully, like someone on the mend. I stepped in and hugged them from the other side, leaning my cheek across the top of Alex's head.

Somewhere outside our huddle, a voice shouted "Gaaaay." It might have been Arturo or DuPree. We ignored them. I guess when you've faced down a greater demon, what some jerk thinks about your sexuality matters about as much as something you can't bother to come up with a simile for.

Sage arrived as we were breaking up our hug. She smacked me on the rear end and said, "Good game." The others ran away and she chased them with the threat of similar treatment.

I walked toward the school, smiling but feeling a thrill of fear as I passed the courtyard where we'd been cornered not much more than 12 hours earlier. Inside, I turned into the side hall where Susan's locker was. She stood in front of it surrounded by her friends. I swallowed hard. I kept limping forward, no matter how much I wanted to turn around.

I didn't stop until I was standing right in front of Susan. Her friends stared at me with open mouths until Tasha shooed them off. She stuck her tongue out as she fled around the nearest corner. I waited for Susan to look up at me.

"Susan," I said. What I was about to do felt harder and scarier than all the things I'd had to do the night before, but I cared about Susan. She deserved this. It was time to live up to my name. Time to be loyal.

"Susan, I'm sorry."

ABOUT THE AUTHOR

Jason Brick started wrestling just after his 11th birthday. He has studied and taught martial arts for the thirty-plus years between now and then. His fascination with Japanese mythology began while training in karate and magnified while living in Japan. When not writing or practicing, he cooks, plays table-top games and tries hard to spoil his wife, two sons and cats in the lush and rainy Pacific Northwest.

28450272R00169

Made in the USA
Charleston, SC
09 April 2014